Books by Gore Vidal

Novels

WILLIWAW
IN A YELLOW WOOD
THE CITY AND THE PILLAR
THE SEASON OF COMFORT
A SEARCH FOR THE KING
DARK GREEN, BRIGHT RED
THE JUDGMENT OF PARIS
MESSIAH
JULIAN
WASHINGTON, D.C.
MYRA BRECKINRIDGE

Short Stories

A THIRSTY EVIL

Plays

VISIT TO A SMALL PLANET
THE BEST MAN

Essays

ROCKING THE BOAT

Myra
Breckinridge

Myra Breckinridge

by GORE VIDAL

LITTLE, BROWN AND COMPANY · BOSTON · TORONTO

LIBRARY OF CONGRESS CATALOG CARD NO. 68-14745

SECOND PRINTING

Published simultaneously in Canada
by Little, Brown & Company (Canada) Limited

PRINTED IN THE UNITED STATES OF AMERICA

For Christopher Isherwood

Myra
Breckinridge

1

I am Myra Breckinridge whom no man will ever possess. Clad only in garter belt and one dress shield, I held off the entire elite of the Trobriand Islanders, a race who possess no words for "why" or "because." Wielding a stone axe, I broke the arms, the limbs, the balls of their finest warriors, my beauty blinding them, as it does all men, unmanning them in the way that King Kong was reduced to a mere simian whimper by beauteous Fay Wray whom I resemble left three-quarter profile if the key light is no more than five feet high during the close shot.

2

The novel being dead, there is no point to writing made-up stories. Look at the French who will not and the Americans who cannot. Look at me who ought not, if only because I exist entirely outside the usual human experience . . . outside and yet wholly relevant for I am the New Woman whose astonishing history is a poignant amalgam of vulgar dreams and knife-sharp realities (shall I ever be free of the dull lingering pain that is my peculiar glory, the price so joyously paid for being Myra Breckinridge, whom no man may possess except on her . . . *my* terms!). Yet not even I can create a fictional character as one-dimensional as the average reader. Nevertheless, I intend to create a literary masterpiece in much the same way that I created myself, and for much the same reason: because it is not there. And I shall accomplish this by presenting you, the reader (as well as Dr. Randolph Spenser Montag, my analyst, friend and dentist, who has proposed that I write in this notebook as therapy), with an exact, literal sense of what it is like, from moment to moment, to be me, what it is like to possess superbly shaped breasts reminiscent of those sported by Jean Harlow in *Hell's Angels* and seen at their best four minutes after the start of the second reel. What it is like to possess perfect thighs with hips resembling that archetypal mandolin from which the male principle draws forth music with prick of flesh so akin — in this metaphor — to pick of celluloid, *blessed* celluloid upon which have been imprinted in our century all the dreams and shadows that have haunted the human race since man's harsh and turbulent origins (quote Lévi-Strauss). Myra Breckinridge is a dish, and never forget it, you motherfuckers, as the children say nowadays.

3

I shall not begin at the beginning since there is no beginning, only a middle into which you, fortunate reader, have just strayed, still uncertain as to what will be done to you in the course of our common voyage to my interior. No, to *our* interior. For we are, at least in the act of this creation, as one, each trapped in time: you later, I now, carefully, thoughtfully forming letters to make words to make sentences.

I shall begin by putting my cards on the table. At this moment (writing the word "moment"), I am not the same Myra Breckinridge who was the scourge of the Trobriand Islanders. She is a creature of fantasy, a daydream revealing the feminine principle's need to regain once more that primacy she lost at the time of the Bronze Age when the cock-worshipping Dorians enslaved the West, impiously replacing *the* Goddess with a god. Happily his days are nearly over; the phallus cracks; the uterus opens; and I am at last ready to begin my mission which is to re-create the sexes and thus save the human race from certain extinction. Meanwhile, I live no longer in the usual world. I have forsaken the familiar. And soon, by an extreme gesture, I shall cease altogether to be human and become legend like Jesus, Buddha, Cybele.

But my immediate task is to impress upon you how disturbingly beautiful I am with large breasts hanging free, for I am wearing nothing but black mesh panties in this overheated room, whose windows I have shut because it is the rush hour (6:07 P.M., Thursday, January 10) and beneath my window the Strip (Sunset Boulevard in Hollywood, California) is filled with noisy cars, barely moving through air so dark with carbon monoxide that one can almost hear in the drivers' lungs the cancer cells as they gaily proliferate like spermatozoa in a healthy boy's testicles.

4

From where I sit, without turning my head, I can see a window covered by venetian blinds. The fourth slat from the bottom is missing and so provides me with a glimpse of the midsection of the huge printed plaster chorus girl who holds a sombrero in one hand as she revolves slowly in front of the Château Marmont where Greta Garbo stays on her rare visits to Hollywood. The window is set in a white wall on which a damp splotch resembles an upside-down two-leaf clover — or heart — or male scrotum as viewed from behind. But no metaphors. Nothing is *like* anything else. Things are themselves entirely and do not need interpretation, only a minimal respect for their precise integrity. The mark on the wall is two feet three inches wide and four feet eight and a fraction inches high. Already I have failed to be completely accurate. I must write "fraction" because I can't read the little numbers on the ruler without my glasses which I never wear.

5

I am certain that I can eventually capture the reality of Myra Breckinridge, despite the treachery and inadequacy of words. I must show you as I am, at this instant, seated at a small card table with two cigarette burns at the edge; one is about the size of a quarter, the other the size of a dime. The second is perhaps the result of a burning ash, while the first . . . But there is to be no speculation, only simple facts, simply stated. I sit now, perspiring freely, the odor of my lovely body is like that of new bread (just one metaphor, then I shall be stylistically pure), mingled with a subtle ammoniac smell that I find nearly as irresistible as all men do. In addition to my extraordinary physical presence, I studied the classics (in translation) at the New School, the contemporary French novel on my own, and I learned German last year in order to understand the films of the Thirties when UFA was a force to be reckoned with.

Now, at this arbitrary instant in time, my hand **moves**

across the page of an oblong black notebook containing three hundred blue-lined pages. I have covered eighteen pages already; that leaves two hundred eighty-two yet to be filled, if one counts the present page of which I have used twelve of thirty-two lines — thirteen with these last words, now fourteen. The hand is small, with delicate tapering fingers and a slight golden down at the back near the wrist. The nails are exquisitely cared for (lacquered silver) except for the right index fingernail, which is cracked diagonally from the left side of the tip to the part where the flesh begins, the result of trying to pry loose an ice cube from one of those new plastic ice trays which so freeze that unless you half melt them under the hot-water tap you can never get the ice out.

There are limits, however, to describing exactly what I see as I write and you read. More to the point, one must accept the fact that there are no words to describe for you *exactly* what my body is like as I sit, perspiring freely, in this furnished room high above the Strip for which I am paying $87.50 a month, much too much, but I must not complain for a life dream has come true. I am in Hollywood, California, the source of all this century's legends, and tomorrow it has been arranged for me to visit Metro-Goldwyn-Mayer! No pilgrim to Lourdes can experience what I know I shall experience once I have stepped into that magic world which has occupied all my waking thoughts for twenty years. Yes, twenty years. Believe it or not, I am twenty-seven years old and saw my first movie at the age of seven: *Marriage Is a Private Affair*, starring Lana Turner, James Craig and the late John Hodiak; produced by Pandro S. Berman and directed by Robert Leonard.

As a small girl I used to yearn for Lana Turner to crush me against her heavy breasts, murmuring, "I love you, Myra, you perfect darling!" Fortunately this Lesbian phase passed and my desires were soon centered upon James Craig. I saw every film he ever made. I even have recordings of his voice. In Parker Tyler's masterpiece *Magic and Myth of the Movies*, he refers to James Craig's voice as "some kind of Middle Southwest drawl, a genuine lulu." I can certify that James Craig was in every way a lulu and for years I practiced self-abuse thinking of that voice, those shoulders, those powerful thighs thrust between my own and, if I may be candid, no matter what condition James Craig is in today, married or not, decrepit or not, Myra Breckinridge is ready to give him a good time for old times' sake.

6

Buck Loner is not the man he was when he was the Singin' Shootin' Cowboy of radio fame — movies too: he made eighteen low-budget westerns and for a time was right up there with Roy Rogers and Gene Autry. In those old movies he appeared to be lean and tough with slender hips and practically no ass at all which I don't find entirely attractive. I like a curve to the masculine buttock, on the order, say, of Tim Holt's in *The Magnificent Ambersons*. Mr. Holt, incidentally, decrepit or not, has a good time coming his way if Myra Breckinridge should happen to cross his path as she is bound to do now that Hollywood is finally, literally, at her feet (lovely feet with a high instep and naturally rosy heels, fit for any fetishist).

Today Buck Loner (born Ted Percey in Portland, Maine) is fat — no, *gross!* — with breasts even larger than mine. He is huge and disgusting and old, and obviously dying to get me into bed even though I am the recent widow of his only nephew Myron Breckinridge, the film critic, who drowned last year while crossing over to Staten Island on the ferry. Did Myron take his own life, you will ask? Yes and no is my answer. Beyond that my lips are sealed. . . . In any case, let us abandon *that* daydream in order to record the hard facts of this morning's encounter with my husband's uncle, Buck Loner.

"Never knew that boy of Gertrude's had such an eye for feminine pulchritude." This sentence drawled in the once famous Buck Loner manner was, I fear, the first thing he said to me as he helped me into a chair beside his redwood desk, one coarse redwood hand lingering for just a moment too long on my left shoulder, in order to ascertain whether or not I was wearing a bra. I was.

"Mr. Loner," I began in a careful low-pitched voice, modeled on that of the late Ann Sheridan (fifth reel of *Doughgirls*). "I will come straight to the point. I need your help."

That was the wrong thing to say. To ask for anything is always the wrong way to begin a conversation but I am not one to beat about a bush, even a bush as unappetizing as Buck Loner. He sat back in his steel and black leather chair, a very expensive item selling for about four hundred dollars at the best office supply stores. I know. I worked one entire year at Abercrombie and Fitch, and so got an idea of just how expensive nice things can be. That was the year poor Myron was trying to complete his book on Parker Tyler and the films of the Forties — a book I intend to finish one day, with or without Mr. Tyler's assistance. Why? Because Tyler's vision (films are the unconscious expressions of age-old human myths) is perhaps the only important critical insight this century has produced. Also, Tyler's close scrutiny of the films of the Forties makes him our age's central thinker, if only because *in the decade between 1935 and 1945, no irrelevant film was made in the United States.* During those years, the entire range of human (which is to say, American) legend was put on film, and any profound study of those extraordinary works is bound to make crystal-clear the human condition. For instance, to take an example at random, Johnny Weissmuller, the zahftic Tarzan, still provides the last word on the subject of soft man's relationship to hard environment . . . that glistening overweight body set against a limestone cliff at noon says the whole thing. Auden once wrote an entire poem praising limestone, unaware that any one of a thousand frames from *Tarzan and the Amazons* (1945) had not only anticipated him but made irrelevant his efforts. This was one of Myron's insights that most excited me. How I miss him.

"How I miss him, Mr. Loner. Particularly now. You see, he didn't leave a penny . . ."

"No insurance, savings account, stocks, bonds, safety deposit box maybe? Gertrude must've left the boy *something.*"

Buck fell into my trap. "No," I said, in a throaty voice with a small croak to it not unlike (but again not *really* like) that of the late Margaret Sullavan. "Gertrude, as you call her, Myron's angel mother, did not leave him one penny. All that she owned on the day she died, Christmas Eve 1966, was a set of bedroom furniture. Ev-

erything else was gone, due to a series of expensive ill-
nesses in the family, hers, Myron's, my own. I won't
bore you with the details but for the last five years we
supported a dozen doctors. Now Gertrude, your sister, is
gone with no one to mourn her at Frank E. Campbell's
Funeral Church except Myron and me. Then he died and
now I'm absolutely alone, and penniless."

During this recital Buck Loner directed toward me
that same narrow-eyed gaze one detects in photographs
of President Johnson whenever he is being asked a question about Bobby Kennedy. But confident in the efficacy
of my ultimate weapon, I merely offered him a sad smile
in return, and blinked a tear or two loose from my Max
Factor Supreme eyelashes. I then looked up at the life-
size photograph in color of Elvis Presley which hangs behind Buck's desk, flanked by two American flags, and
began my pitch. "Mr. Loner, Gertrude, Myron's
mother . . ."

"A marvelous woman . . ." he began huskily but no
man alive can outdo *me* in the huskiness department.

"Gertrude," I positively *rasped* through a Niagara of
tears unshed, "with her dying breath, or one of her dying
breaths — we missed a lot of what she said toward the
end because of the oxygen tent and the fact she could not
wear her teeth — Gertrude said, 'Myron — and you
too, angel girl — if anything happens to me and you ever
need help, go to your Uncle Ted, go to Buck Loner and
remind that son-of-a-bitch' — I am now quoting verba-
tim — 'that the property in Westwood just outside of
Hollywood where he has his Academy of Drama and
Modeling was left to us jointly by our father whose or-

ange grove it was in the Twenties, and you tell that bastard' — I'm sorry but you know how Gertrude talked,
those years as a practical nurse left their toll — 'that I
have a copy of the will and I want my share to go to you,
Myron, because that property must be worth a good million bucks by now!' " I stopped, as though too moved by
my own recital to continue.

Buck Loner idly stroked the bronze bust of Pat Boone
which serves as the base for his desk lamp. A long moment passed. I studied the office, admired its rich appointments, realizing that half of the ground it stood on
— some fifty acres of Westwood's finest residential
property — was mine. The proof was in my purse: a
photostat of Buck Loner's father's will.

"Gertrude was always a high-spirited gal, ever since
she was yea-high." He indicated what looked to be a
Shetland pony; on one finger a huge diamond glittered.
"Poor Gertrude died most horribly, Myron wrote me.
Great suffering at the end." He smacked his lips, the un-
mitigated shit, but cool it, Myra baby, I said to myself,
and half of all this will be yours. Sudden daydream:
Buck Loner hanging upside down like a fat sack of potatoes while yours truly works him over with a tennis
racket strung with copper wires.

"I never knew Myron," he added, as though this might
somehow make spurious the relationship.

"Myron never knew you." I was deliberately redundant. "I mean he used to follow your career with interest, collected all sorts of stories about you from the old
Radio Times. And of course you were to have figured at
some length in one of the chapters of his book *Parker*

Tyler and the Films of the Forties; or, the Transcendental Pantheon."

"How about that?" Buck Loner looked pleased, as well he ought to be. "I suppose my nephew left a will?"

I was ready for that one. I told him that I possessed three wills. His father's leaving the orange grove jointly to Gertrude and himself, Gertrude's leaving her share of the Westwood property to Myron, and Myron's leaving his entire estate to me.

Buck Loner sighed. "You know," he said, "the school ain't doin' too well." Phonetically that is not exactly what he said, but it is close. I am fortunate in having no gift at all for characterizing in prose the actual speech of others and so, for literary purposes, I prefer to make everyone sound like me. Therefore I shall make no further effort to reproduce Buck Loner's speech, except when something particularly vivid stays with me. Nothing vivid was said for some minutes while he lied to me about the financial status of the Academy of Drama and Modeling. But of course everyone in show business knows that the Academy is a huge success with an enrollment of one thousand three hundred young men and women, all studying to be actors, singers, models. Some live on campus but most live elsewhere and drive to school in their jalopies (a marvelous Forties word that I heard for the first time in *Best Foot Forward* — oh, to have been an adult in those years!). The Academy mints money.

When Buck had finished his tale of woe, I crossed my legs slowly and deliberately (my skirt was practically mini, my legs divine), and was rewarded by a noticeable increase in Buck's salivation. He swallowed hard, eyes on that triangulated darkness beneath the skirt, forever inviting the question: is it you-know-what or panties? Let him wonder! No man will ever possess Myra Breckinridge, though she will possess men, in her own good time and in ways convenient to her tyrannous lust. In any case, Buck Loner is a three-time married man whose current wife, Bobbie Dean, once sang with Claude Thornhill's band in the Forties, and is now a passionate Jehovah's Witness, forever saving sinners in back streets. Gertrude thought her common.

"Naturally, this is all quite sudden, Myra, I may call you Myra? Even though we never met but then you are my niece-in-law, and so practically kissin' kin."

There is a crash outside my window — was a crash (in the time I took to write "there is a crash" the tense changed). Two cars have collided on the Strip. I heard breaking glass. Now I hear nothing. If the accident was serious there will soon be the sound of a siren. More than ever am I convinced that the only useful form left to literature in the post-Gutenberg age is the memoir: the absolute truth, copied precisely from life, preferably at the moment it is happening . . .

Buck Loner made me an offer. While his lawyer and my lawyer work out a settlement, he would be happy to give me a job starting now and extending until the school year ends in June and all the talent scouts from TV, movie and recording companies converge upon the Academy to observe the students do their stuff. I accepted his offer. Why not? I need a place to live (as well as an entrée into the world of the movies), and so what could be better than a teaching job at the Academy? I will also enjoy meeting young men (though whether or not they will enjoy meeting me remains to be seen!), and the Academy is crawling with them, arrogant, cocky youths; several whistled at me in the corridor as I made my way to Buck Loner's office. Well, they will suffer for their bad manners! No man may jeer at Myra Breckinridge with impunity!

"Now we have an opening for you in our Acting Department — that's for movie and TV acting, we don't go in for stage-type acting, no real demand . . ."

"The theatre is finished . . ." I began.

"You can say that again." It was plain that he was not interested in my theories which reflect more or less Myron's thesis that this century's only *living* art form is the movies. I say more or less because though I agree with Myron that the films of the 1940's are superior to all the works of the so-called Renaissance, including Shakespeare and Michelangelo, I have been drawn lately to the television commercial which, though in its rude infancy, shows signs of replacing all the other visual arts. But my ideas are not yet sufficiently formulated to record them here, suffice it to say that the placing of the man in the driver's seat (courtesy of Hertz) reveals in a most cogent way man's eternal need for mastery over both space and distance, a never-ending progress that began in the caves at Lascaux and continues, even as I write, in the Apollo capsule with its mixed oxygen environment.

"Your work load will of course be light. After all, you're a member of the family and of course I'm taking into account your terrible recent loss, though it has been my experience that work distracts our attention from

grief in a most extraordinary way." While he was filibus-
tering, he was studying a chart. He then scribbled a note
and gave it to me. On Monday, Thursday and Saturday
mornings I am to give an hour course in Empathy. Tues-
day and Friday afternoons I teach Posture.

"You seem particularly well equipped to give the
course in Posture. I couldn't help but notice how you
looked when you entered the room, you carry yourself
like a veritable queen. As for Empathy, it is the Sign
Kwa Known [*sine qua non*] of the art of film acting."

We sparred with one another, each lying to beat the
band. He so pleased to have me "on the team" and me so
happy to be able to work in Hollywood, California, a
life's dream come true and — as they used to say in the
early Sixties — all that jazz. Oh, we are a pair of jolly
rogues! He means to cheat me out of my inheritance
while I intend to take him for every cent he's got, as well
as make him fall madly in love just so, at the crucial moment, I can kick his fat ass in, fulfilling the new pattern
to which I am now irrevocably committed. Or as
Diotima said to Hyperion, in Hölderlin's novel, "It was
no man that you wanted, believe me; you wanted a
world." I too want a world and mean to have it. This
man — any man — is simply a means of getting it
(which is Man).

There goes the siren. The accident was serious. I
stretch my legs. The left foot's asleep. In a moment I
shall put down the yellow ballpoint pen, get to my feet,
experience briefly pins and needles; then go to the window and lift the blind and see if there are dead bodies in
the street. Will there be blood? I dread it. Truly.

BUCK LONER REPORTS —
Recording Disc No. 708 —
10 January
           Other matters to be taken up by board in reference to purchases for new closed cir cuit TV period paragraph I sort of remember that Gertrudes boy was married some years ago and I recall being surprised as he was a fag or so I always thought with that sister of mine for a mother how could he not be only thing is I never knew the little bastard except one meeting in St Louis oh maybe twenty years ago when she was there with her third husband the certified public accountant and I re member vaguely this sissy kid who wanted to go to the movies all the time who I gave an autographed picture of me on Sporko that palomino horse that was and is the trademark of Buck Loner even though the original palomino in question has been for a long time up there in the happy hunting ground and my ass is now too big to inflict on any other nag except maybe Myra Breckinridge period

paragraph what is the true Myra Breckinridge story
that is the big question you could have knocked me
over with a feather when she came sashaying into
the office with her skirt hiked up damn near to her
chin at least when she sits down she is a good look
ing broad but hoteyed definitely hoteyed and pos
sibly mentally unbalanced I must keep an eye on
her in that department but the tits are keen and
probably hers and I expect she is just hungering for
the old Buck Loner Special parenthesis start taking
pee-pills again to lose weight zipper keeps slipping
down which makes a damned sloppy impression end
parenthesis period paragraph but what I dont like
one bit is the matter of the will and I guess I better
put Flagler and Flagler onto it first thing tomorrow
it is true that the property was left me and Gertrude
jointly but she always said Ted she said she never
called me Buck she was the most envious broad that
ever lived especially when I was right up there big
gest star of them all after Roy bigger than Gene cer
tainly but wish I had Genes eye for real estate that
man is loaded of course I dont do so bad with the
Academy but Gene Autry today is capital r capital i
capital c capital h rich well I was better box office
Ted Gertrude said you can keep my share of that
lousy orange grove that our father threw away his
life savings to buy just as the bottom dropped out of
citrus fruit I never want to see or hear of it again
is what she said more or less but naturally when
word come to Saint Louis and later to the Island of
Manhattan where she was living with that crazy pic
ture painter that Hollywood was spilling over into
nearby Brentwood and Westwood and all the other
woods were filling up with lovers of the sun and fun
from all parts of the U S A Gertrude did ask once or
twice about our mutual holding but when I told her I

needed money to start the Academy and needed the
orange grove to teach in and maybe put a building
on she was very reasonable merely saying that when
the time came I was to help Myron to become a
movie star as he was even better looking than I was
at his age and besides could act the little fag she
sent me all sorts of pictures of him and he was
pretty as a picture in a drippy sort of way and wrote
these far out pieces about the movies that I could
never get through in magazines I never heard of in
England and even in French some of them were
written I will say he sent them all to me including
a long article type piece that I did read about so help
me god the rear ends of all the major cowboy stars
from austere aspiring Gothic flat ass Hoot Gibson
to impertinent baroque ass James Garner shit ex
clamation mark paragraph Flagler and Flagler will
be notified first thing tomorrow morning and told to
examine with a fine tooth comb the deeds to this
property and also to make a careful investigation
of one Myra Breckinridge widow and claimant and
try to find some loophole as I have no intention at
all of letting her horn in on a property that I my
self increased in value from a five thousand dollar
orange grove to what is now at a conservative esti
mate worth in the neighborhood counting buildings
of course of two million dollars maybe I should lay
Myra that might keep her happy for a while while
we discuss the ins and outs of our business mean
while I better see if that fag nephew of mine left a
proper will all this will have to be gone into in care
ful detail by Flagler and Flagler and their private
detective meanwhile she will be working here where
I can keep an eye on her period paragraph check
new TV makeup equipment write President Johnson
giving him my views on subsidy for the arts in line

with talk I gave to Fresno Rotary before Xmas those
two kids are definitely balling and I don't like that
sort of thing to be too visible on the campus par
ticularly since she lives here in the dormitory and
the matron tells me she is off with that stud every
chance she can get and is always coming in after
midnight a beautiful little piece she is and it may
well be that the Buck Loner Special could straighten
her out but I must proceed cautiously like they say
as she is a minor of eighteen and naturally drawn
to a male minor of nineteen six feet two and built
like a stone wall who wants to be a movie star with
sideburns a nice kid if he stays out of jail and I hope
one day he makes it but meanwhile its his making
her that I mind I mean what would her mother say
her worst fears about Hollywood fulfilled I better
tell the matron to give her a tough talking to or back
she goes to Winnipeg as an enemy alien and deflow
ered virgin through no fault of yours truly remem
ber to tell masseuse to come at five instead of six
am getting horny as hell thinking about the dear
little thing from Winnipeg whats her name Sally
Sue Baby Dee Mary Ann thats it Mary Ann Pringle
and shes making it with Rusty Godowsky from De
troit where else a nice dumb polack who maybe has
that extra something that makes for stardom that
masseuse better be good today

7

I write this sitting at my desk in the office to which I have been assigned in the west wing of the main building of what must be an incredibly valuable piece of real estate. I've spent the last few days prowling about the Academy and it's a most expensive creation, worth millions I should say, and half of it's mine, or at least half the ground it stands on. I have already contacted a good lawyer and presently he will surprise Buck Loner with my claims. Our case, I am assured, is airtight.

I find Buck Loner something of an enigma. No man can be as cheerful as he seems to be, as desirous of creating love as he says he is. Yet it is true that oceans of warmth flow from him to all the students, quite indiscriminately, and they seem to adore him, even those who are known as "hippies" and mock everyone (the argot is curiously rich out here, and slightly repellent: teenagers — already a ghastly word — are known as "teeny-boppers"!). Reluctantly, I find myself admiring the man, monster though he is. But then I shall soon break him to my will. Is there a man alive who is a match for Myra Breckinridge?

8

I sit now in a bus on my way to Culver City — and Metro-Goldwyn-Mayer! My heart is beating so quickly that I can hardly bear to look out the window for fear that suddenly against that leaden horizon marked by oil derricks, I shall behold — like some fantastic palace of dreams — the Irving Thalberg Memorial Building and its attendant sound stages whose blank (but oh so evocative!) façades I have studied in photographs for twenty years.

Not wanting to spoil my first impression, I keep my eye on this notebook which I balance on one knee as I put down at random whatever comes into my mind, simply anything in order to save for myself the supreme moment of ecstasy when the Studio of Studios, the sublime motor to this century's myths, appears before me as it has so many times in dreams, its great doors swinging wide to welcome Myra Breckinridge to her rightful kingdom.

I was born to be a star, and look like one today: a false hairpiece gives body to my hair while the light Max Factor base favored by Merle Oberon among other screen lovelies makes luminous my face even in the harsh light of a sound stage where I shall soon be standing watching a take. Then when the director says, "O.K., print it," and the grips prepare for another setup, the director will notice me and ask my name and then take me into the commissary and there, over a Green Goddess salad (a favorite of the stars), talk to me at length about my face, wondering whether or not it is photogenic until I stop him with a smile and say: "There is only one way to find out. A screen test." To be a film star is my dearest daydream. After all, I have had some practical experience in New York. Myron and I both appeared in a number of underground movies. Of course they were experimental films and like most experiments, in the laboratory and out, they failed but even had they succeeded they could never have been truly Hollywood, truly mythic. Nevertheless, they gave me a sense of what it must be like to be a star.

This trip is endless. I hate buses. I must rent or buy a car. The distances are unbelievable out here and to hire a taxi costs a fortune. This particular section of town is definitely ratty-looking with dingy bungalows and smog-filled air; my eyes burn and water. Fortunately elaborate neon signs and an occasional eccentrically shaped building make magic of the usual. We are now passing a diner in the shape of an enormous brown doughnut. I feel better already. Fantasy has that effect on me.

What to make of the students? I have now taught four

classes in Posture (how to walk gracefully and sit down without knocking over furniture) and two in Empathy (I invite them to pretend they are oranges, drinks of water, clouds . . . the results are unusual, to say the least).

Though I have nothing to do with the Speech Department, I could not help but notice what difficulty most of the students have in talking. The boys tend to bark while the girls whine through their noses. Traditional human speech seems to have passed them by, but then one must never forget that they are the first creations of that television culture which began in the early Fifties. Their formative years were spent watching pale gray figures (no blacks, no whites — significant detail) move upon a twenty-one-inch screen. As a result, they are bland and inattentive, responsive only to the bold rhythms of commercials. Few can read anything more complex than a tabloid newspaper. As for writing, it is enough that they can write their name, or "autograph" as they are encouraged to call it, anticipating stardom. Nevertheless, a few have a touch of literary genius (that never dies out entirely), witness the obscene graffiti on the men's bathroom wall into which I strayed by accident the first day and saw, in large letters over one of the urinals, "Buck Sucks." Can this be true? I would put nothing past a man who traffics so promiscuously in love, not knowing that it is hate alone which inspires us to action and makes for civilization. Look at Juvenal, Pope, Billy Wilder.

In the Posture class I was particularly struck by one of the students, a boy with a Polish name. He is tall with a great deal of sand-colored curly hair and sideburns; he has pale blue eyes with long black lashes and a curving mouth on the order of the late Richard Cromwell, so satisfyingly tortured in *Lives of a Bengal Lancer*. From a certain unevenly rounded thickness at the crotch of his blue jeans, it is safe to assume that he is marvelously hung. Unfortunately he is hot for an extremely pretty girl with long straight blonde hair (dyed), beautiful legs and breasts, reminiscent of Lupe Velez. She is mentally retarded. When I asked her to rise she did not recognize the word "rise" and so I had to ask her "to get up" which she did understand. He is probably just as stupid but fortunately has the good sense not to talk too much. When he does, however, he puts on a hillbilly accent that is so authentic that I almost melt in my drawers.

"I thank we gawn git on mahty fahn, Miz Myra" were his first words to me after class as he looked down into my upturned face, confident of his masculine primacy. He was, in fact, so close to me that I could smell the most appetizing odor of deodorant mingled with tobacco and warm boy. But before I could make a suitable answer, *she* pulled him away. Poor child! She doesn't know that I shall have him in the end while

9

I can hardly bear it another moment! I am reborn or in the process of rebirth like Robert Montgomery in *Here Comes Mr. Jordan*.

I am seated in front of a French café in a Montmartre street on the back lot at Metro. Last year's fire destroyed many of the studio's permanent outdoor sets — those streets and castles I knew so much better than ever I knew the Chelsea area of Manhattan where Myron and I used to exist. I deeply regret the fire, mourn all that was lost, particularly the famous New York City street of brownstones and the charming village in Normandy. But, thank Heaven, this café still stands. Over a metal framework, cheap wood has been so arranged and painted as to suggest with astonishing accuracy a Paris bistro, complete with signs for BYRRH, while a striped awning shades metal tables and chairs set out on the "sidewalk." Any minute now, I expect to see Parisians. I would certainly like to see a waiter and order a Pernod.

I can hardly believe that I am sitting at the same table where Audrey Hepburn once awaited Gene Kelly so many years ago, and I can almost re-create for myself the lights, the camera, the sound boom, the technicians, all converged upon this one table where, in a blaze of artificial sunlight, Audrey — much too thin but a lovely face with eyes like mine — sits and waits for her screen lover while a man from makeup delicately dusts those famous features with powder.

From the angle where I sit I can see part of the street in Carvel where Andy Hardy lived. The street is beautifully kept up as the shrine it is, a last memorial to all that was touching and — yes — good in the American past, an era whose end was marked by two mushroom shapes set like terminal punctuation marks against the Asian sky.

A few minutes ago I saw Judge Hardy's house with its neatly tended green lawn and windows covered with muslin behind which there is nothing at all. It is quite eerie the way in which the houses look entirely real from every angle on the slightly curving street with its tall green trees and flowering bushes. Yet when one walks around to the back of the houses, one sees the rusted metal framework, the unpainted wood which has begun to rot, the dirty glass of the windows and the muslin curtains soiled and torn. Time withers all things human; although yesterday evening when I saw Ann Rutherford, stopped in her car at a red light, I recognized immediately the great black eyes and the mobile face. She at least endures gallantly, and I could not have been more thrilled! Must find where Lewis Stone is buried.

This is the happiest moment of my life, sitting here alone on the back lot with no one in sight, for I was able to escape the studio guide by telling him that I wanted to lie down in an empty office of the Thalberg Building; then of course I flew straight here to the back lot which is separated from the main studio by a public road.

If only Myron could have seen this! Of course he would have been saddened by the signs of decay. The spirit of what used to be has fled. Most dreadful of all, NO FILM is currently being made on the lot; and that means that the twenty-seven huge sound stages which saw the creation of so many miracles: Gable, Garbo, Hepburn (Katharine), Powell, Loy, Garland, Tracy and James Craig are now empty except for a few crews making television commercials.

Yet I must write the absolute truth for I am not Myron Breckinridge but myself and despite the intensely symbiotic relationship my husband and I enjoyed during his brief life and despite the fact that I do entirely support his thesis that the films of 1935 to 1945 inclusive were the high point of Western culture, completing what began that day in the theatre of Dionysos when Aeschylus first spoke to the Athenians, I must confess that I part company with Myron on the subject of TV. Even before Marshall McLuhan, I was drawn to the gray shadows of the cathode tube. In fact, I was sufficiently *avant-garde* in 1959 to recognize the fact that it was no longer the movies but the television commercial that engaged the passionate attention of the world's best artists and technicians. And now the result of their extraordinary artistry is this new world, like it or not, we are liv-

ing in: post-Gutenberg and pre-Apocalypse. For almost
twenty years the minds of our children have been filled
with dreams that will stay with them forever, the way
those maddening jingles do (as I write, I have begun
softly to whistle "Rinso White," a theme far more meaningful culturally than all of Stravinsky or even John
Cage). I submitted a piece on this subject to the *Partisan
Review* in the summer of 1960. I believe, without false
modesty, that I proved conclusively that the relationship
between consumer and advertiser is the last demonstration of *necessary* love in the West, and its principal form
of expression is the television commercial. I never heard
from *PR* but I kept a carbon of the piece and will incor-
porate it into the book on Parker Tyler, perhaps as an
appendix.

For almost an hour I watched a television commercial
being made on the same stage where Bette Davis acted in
The Catered Affair — that predictably unhappy result
of the movies attempting to take over the television
drama when what they should have taken over was the
spirit of the commercials. Then I was given lunch in the
commissary which is much changed since the great days
when people in extraordinary costumes wandered about,
creating the impression that one was inside a time machine gone berserk. Now television executives and technicians occupy all the tables and order what used to be
Louis B. Mayer Chicken Soup only the name of Mayer
has been, my guide told me, stricken from the menu. So
much for greatness! Even more poignant as reminders of
human transiency are the empty offices on the second
floor of the Thalberg Building. I was particularly upset

to see that the adjoining suites of Pandro S. Berman and
the late Sam Zimbalist were both vacant. Zimbalist (immortal because of *Boom Town*) died in Rome while pro-
ducing *Ben Hur* which saved the studio's bacon, and
Pandro S. Berman (*Dragon Seed, The Picture of Dorian
Gray, The Seventh Cross*) has gone into what the local
trade papers refer to as "indie production." How tragic!
MGM without Pandro S. Berman is like the American
flag without its stars.

No doubt about it, an era has indeed ended and I am its
chronicler. Farewell the classic films, hail the television
commercial! Yet nothing human that is great can entirely
end. It is merely transmuted — in the way that the
wharf where Jeanette MacDonald arrived in New Or-
leans (*Naughty Marietta*, 1935) has been used over and
over again for a hundred other films even though it will
always remain, to those who have a sense of history,
Jeanette's wharf. Speaking of history, there was something curiously godlike about Nelson Eddy's recent death
before a nightclub audience at Miami. In the middle of a
song, he suddenly forgot the words. And so, in that plan-
gent baritone which long ago earned him a permanent
place in the pantheon of superstars, he turned to his ac-
companist and said, "Play 'Dardanella,' and maybe I'll remember the words." Then he collapsed and died.

Play "Dardanella"! Play on! In any case, one must be
thankful for those strips of celluloid which still endure to
remind us that once there were gods and goddesses in our
midst and Metro-Goldwyn-Mayer (where I now sit)
preserved their shadows for all time! Could the actual
Christ have possessed a fraction of the radiance and the

mystery of H. B. Warner in the first *King of Kings* or
revealed, even on the cross, so much as a shadow of the
moonstruck Nemi-agony of Jeffrey Hunter in the second *King of Kings,* that astonishing creation of Nicholas
Ray?

10

Seated at a table in the Academy cafeteria. It is three weeks to the day since I arrived. People want to sit with me, but I graciously indicate that I would rather make these notes. They respect my writing at odd times in public places. There is a rumor that I am with the CIA.

While waiting just now to be served today's lunch specialty, a chili con carne that looks suspiciously like Gravy Train, a concentrated dog food which California's poverty-stricken Mexicans mix with their beans, I noticed, as always with a certain pleasure, the way the students go about playing at stardom.

A fantastically beautiful girl called Gloria Gordon holds court at one table, wearing a silver lamé evening gown, cut to the navel, while rock-and-roll singers do an impromptu number in the center of the room, to the delight of the western stars in their boots and chaps; a pleasure not shared by the motorcyclists in their black leather, bedecked with swastikas and chains, radiating

hostility, so unlike the Easterners who are solemnly cata-
tonic in their Brooks Brothers suits and button-down col-
lars, each clutching an empty attaché case. The students
regard the Easterners respectfully as being the farthest-
out of all for they are, reputedly, the drug-takers. Of
course all the students smoke pot and experiment with
LSD but only a few main-line, and of those few the Easterners, to a man, are thought to be totally hooked.

As a spiritual child of the Forties, I cannot give my
imprimatur to this sort of behavior. The drug-taker is a
passivist. I am an activist. Yet — to be fair — how can
the average person make a meaningful life for himself in
an overpopulated world? There is very little of interest
for him to do in the way of work, while sex is truly absorbing only for those who possess imagination as well as
means. With these young people one has the sense that
they know instinctively that there are plenty more
where they came from and so why fuss? They'll soon be
gone, their places taken by others so closely resembling
them that only a mother's eye could tell the difference.

They are an anonymous blur, even to themselves,
which explains their fitful, mindless shuffling of roles. In
the morning Gloria will wear a silver lamé gown complete with Miriam Hopkins cocktail shaker; in the evening her ensemble may consist of leotards and a sunbon-
net. It is easy for these young people to be anything since
they are so plainly nothing, and know it. Their meta-
morphoses, however, seldom involve more than a change
of clothes and the affecting of certain speech manner-
isms, appropriated from Western or Eastern stars of

television series, liberally sprinkled with jokes told late at night on television by nightclub comedians.

Mimesis is normal, particularly in youth, and my only demur is that today's models are, by and large, debasing. In the Forties, American boys created a world empire because they chose to be James Stewart, Clark Gable and William Eythe. By imitating godlike autonomous men, our boys were able to defeat Hitler, Mussolini and Tojo. Could we do it again? Are the private eyes and denatured cowboys potent enough to serve as imperial exemplars? No. At best, there is James Bond . . . and he invariably ends up tied to a slab of marble with a blowtorch aimed at his crotch. Glory has fled and only the television commercials exist to remind us of the Republic's early greatness and virile youth.

Of all the students at the Academy, only one has sought to model himself on a Forties star: the sickest of the Easterners is currently playing Humphrey Bogart, and he is hopeless in the part. The rest are entirely contemporary, pretending to be folk singers, cowboys and English movie actors. Needless to say, all attempts at imitating Cockney or Liverpudlian accents fail. For one thing the accents are too much for them; for another, any evidence that there could be a real world *outside* Southern California tends to demoralize our students. Of course they can observe other worlds on television but then that is show business and familiar. Even the Martian landscape of Southeast Asia loses all strangeness when framed by the homey plastic of a television set, while the people involved in that war are quite plainly extras lucky

enough to be called upon to fill in prime airtime with the
appearance of people dying and living.

Naturally, the Vietnam exercise appeals enormously
to the students. "I mean," said one of them, "if we don't
stop them there — you know, where they are now —
they'll be right here in L.A." To which I answered,
"This city could not be worse run by the Chinese than it
is by the present administration and, frankly, if the Chinese could be persuaded to take on the job — which is
doubtful — I think we should let them."

Since that exchange, Myra Breckinridge has been
thought by some to be a Commie, not the worst thing to
be known as at the Academy since the students are scared
to death of Communism (like, man, they make you
work!), and so regard any alleged conspirator or sympa-
thizer with awe . . . which I like. As for the theory of
Communism, they have not a clue. In fact, the only book
any of them has read is something called *The Green Be-
rets,* a jingoistic work written in the spirit of Kipling with
the art of Mickey Spillane. Apparently this work is a
constant source of sadistic reveries. Time and again have
I heard the students speak wistfully of fighting and torturing the Vietcong, or rather of other young men fighting and torturing the Vietcong on their behalf. Not only
are the male students drawn to violence (at second
hand), they are also quite totalitarian-minded, even for
Americans, and I am convinced that any attractive television personality who wanted to become our dictator
would have their full support.

As usual, I am ambivalent. On the one hand, I am intellectually devoted to the idea of the old America. I believe

in justice, I want redress for all wrongs done, I want the good life — if such a thing exists — accessible to all. Yet, emotionally, I would be only too happy to become world dictator, if only to fulfill my mission: *the destruction of the last vestigial traces of traditional manhood in the race in order to realign the sexes, thus reducing population while increasing human happiness and preparing humanity for its next stage.*

No doubt this tension in me constitutes my uniqueness, and genius. Certainly everyone senses it. Students flock to my lectures. Craving my attention and advice, they giggle, fascinated and frightened, at what I say. They sense my power, particularly the boys who are drawn to it even as they fear it. Of course these students are not entirely typical of the nation. They are somewhat stupider than the average, while simultaneously rather more imaginative and prone to daydreaming. Like most members of the lower classes, they are reactionary in the truest sense: the unfamiliar alarms them and since they have had no experience outside what Dr. Montag calls their "peer group," they are, consequently, in a state of near-panic most of the time, reacting against almost everything. It was Myron who observed in 1964 that all of the male hustlers were supporting Goldwater for President. He wrote a fascinating analysis of this phenomenon and sent it to the ADA, but received no reply.

11

There is no denying the fact that Mary-Ann Pringle of Winnipeg is an attractive girl and I plainly dislike the fact since I am jealous of all women though I do not need to be. But then envy is the nature of the human beast and one must face that fact, like all facts. For instance, is it a fact that in my Posture class I have been unnecessarily cruel to Rusty, her boyfriend? Yes. I have been cruel. One must never lie to oneself or, for that matter, to others. No truth should ever be withheld. Without precise notation and interpretation there is only chaos. Essentially, each of us is nothing but a flux of sensations and impressions that only sort themselves out as a result of the most strict analysis and precise formulation, as Robbe-Grillet has proposed but not accomplished (his efforts to revive the novel as an art form are as ineffective as his attempts to destroy the art of film are successful). Of course, a *true* naming of things is impossible. Our minds are too feeble and our sensory equipment is too mys-

terious and complex for us ever to do more than make
approximate definitions. Yet we must continue to make
the effort, no matter how inadequate the result. In fact, I
have made it a rule that whatever I *consciously* experience, I promptly submit to analysis. Take Mary-Ann
Pringle.

I was in my office, just after lunch, looking over my
notes for tomorrow's class in Empathy, when there was a
timid knock at the door (despite my vow never to make
anthropomorphic references in referring to *things* there
was no doubt in my mind, even as I heard that knock,
that it was the result of a fist striking wood directed by a
frightened i.e. timid intelligence).

Mary-Ann entered, wearing miniskirt (bright yellow)
and sweater (dark green) and no bra. She is innocent,
attractive, young. Her hands are those of a child, rather
grubby with broken nails but marvelously smooth, like
seamless gloves.

"Miss Myra, I wanted to know could I talk to you just
a minute. I'm not disturbing you, am I, Miss Myra?"

As much as I dislike girls, particularly beautiful young
ones, I found myself experiencing an emotion which
might be called maternal. I promptly stifled it but was
kind. "Of course you're not disturbing me, Mary-Ann.
My door is always open to you. Sit down. A cigarette? A
Coke?"

I realized too late that I was playing Gail Patrick and
would have to continue flashing brilliant smiles for the
remainder of the two-scene since I seldom abandon a role
once I have embarked upon it. Artistic integrity demands
consistency, even with the unappreciative Mary-Anns of

this world. I would have been much happier playing a sad but compassionate Loretta Young but since I had begun as Gail Patrick I would so remain, grinning doggedly.

After many soft hesitancies, she came to the point: my treatment of Rusty. "You see, he's real sensitive underneath. Oh, I know he doesn't look it being so strong and playing football one year pro and everything, but he's got feelings like anybody else and when you said that he walked 'like an ape with fleas,' well, he was pretty darned upset and so was I."

I looked grave through my smile, not an easy thing to do. "Oh, I'm sorry to hear that. Truly I am. I only wanted to help. And he *does* have terrible posture."

"It's this old football accident he was too shy to tell you about which broke four ribs and when they healed he was sort of ass . . . assy . . ."

"Asymmetrical?"

"That's right, sort of curved to one side. I mean it's not noticeable except when he's nervous and trying to walk straight and you're staring at him and picking on him."

"You make me very, very ashamed, Mary-Ann." I sounded extraordinarily sincere even to my own ears. "He seems like such a strong *confident* young man that I never dreamed he was so sensitive."

"Well, he is about some things. Like that." Mary-Ann looked so forlorn, so touching, so young, so entirely attractive that it was all I could do to keep from taking her in my arms — a gesture bound to be misinterpreted!

Instead I assured her that I would try to curb my natu-

ral impatience in the future. Nevertheless, she must realize that in the teacher-student relationship one must always tell the *total* truth. In this case, though Rusty does
walk like an ape with fleas, I am duty bound to add that
his other bodily movements are often remarkably grace-
ful, the result of a serene and as yet uncompromised old-
fashioned virility which seems never to desert him, except in class when I draw attention to his defects. So I
will, I vowed, remember in the future to mix censure
with deserved praise. She was pleased and grateful.
Lovely Mary-Ann. Is she as stupid as she seems?

12

I had just returned from Empathy II when Buck surged into my office; there is no other verb to describe his entrance. Wearing the white Stetson that is his trademark and the well-cut tweeds that reveal his true businessman's identity, Buck entirely filled the room, his smile positively scarring the air, it was so broad, so happy, so ingenuous.

"Well, li'l lady, you lookin' reel good." No, I must not attempt any further phonetic rendering of his speech which, in any case, shifts so rapidly from Cheyenne to Pomona that one could go mad trying to define its actual provenance. "The kids all love you. Honest they do. I've been getting crackerjack reports from them, particularly in Empathy, and I hope once our little business problem is ironed out, you will consider staying on." He sank into the room's only armchair and gave me a conspiratorial wink. "You got what it takes to be a fine teacher and helper to somebody like me, who's ignorant as a yellow dog."

"Not so ignorant!" Two could play at flattery. By the time I'm finished with Buck Loner, he won't have the proverbial pot to piss in or my name is not Myra Breckinridge, at whose feet the proudest men have groveled, wincing beneath the lash of her scorn, whimpering for a chance to hold in their coarse arms her — my — fragile, too lovely for this world or at least *their* world, body. *I am Woman.* "But I will say that after a week of getting to know your students, I realize at last what overpopulation means. The brains have been bred out of the current generation. They are like the local oranges, all bright appearance and no taste."

I meant to wound. I did. Buck sat back in the chair as though I had struck his great golden autumnal moonface. "Why, that's very, *very* unfair, Myra. Very unfair indeed." He seemed at a complete loss how to begin a defense.

In any case, I did not give him time. "I realize the scandalous state of the public school system in the United States as well as the effect television has had upon the mental processes of those whose childhood was spent staring at the box, and I accept the fact that these young people are a new breed who have gone beyond linear type in their quest for experience — 'knowledge' does not seem to be the right word for what they're after; perhaps the 'easy buck' says it all . . . no play on names intended. Anyway I find it extraordinarily difficult getting through to them even the simplest thought, but since

I am an American brought up during the great age of film, I want to believe that our culture is still alive, still able to create a masterpiece like *Since You Went Away*, and so I must conclude that what you have assembled here are the national dregs, the misfits, the neurotics, the daydreamers, the unrealists, the — in short — fuckups who form a significant minority in our culture, witness what happened November twenty-second, 1963, at Dallas!"

Well, that took the wind out of those sails. He absolutely shrank into his chair, contracted before my eyes. The huge open face shut tight against my imperious gaze. Frankly I can think of no pleasure greater than to approach an open face and swiftly say whatever needs to be said to shut it. Myron disapproved of this trait in me but I believed then, as I do now, that if one is right, the unsayable must be said, and the faces that I temporarily shut will, in the long run, be better faces for the exercise.

Buck did not agree. "These boys and girls are a cross-section of the youth of this country, no better, no worse. What they have got that *is* unusual and which may disqualify them from attending your Business School at Harvard is the overwhelming desire to be in show business, to have their names and faces known to all the world, to see themselves beloved by strangers, and that, believe me, is the only truly gratifying life any human can have, once they get the bug, that is, like I did, and like they have."

"My dear Buck," I addressed him warmly, a husky Jean Arthur note to my voice, *"you* are unusual. Unique. You were — are — a star. You were — and through the

reruns of your old movies on TV, you still are, perma-
nently — beloved. Long after these two bodies, yours
and mine, have gone to dust and this room is gone, and
these boys and girls have all grown old and died and their
descendants come and gone, *you will live.* Buck Loner,
the Singin' Shootin' Radio Cowboy, astride Sporko, will
ride the ranges of the world's imagination. You are for all
time. They are not and never can be."

I had him there. My famous one-two, learned from
Myron: first, excessive flattery with a grain of truth
swathed in cultured nacre; then the lethal puncheroo.
His face reflected ecstasy and dismay. Myra's round.

"Well, honey, I see what you mean and it's a real
subtle point you got there. I mean, yes, I did make eighteen feature-length oaters, that's true, and that bastard
lawyer of mine never put in one word in my contracts
about future resale to the TV even though I once said to
him, 'Sydney, there is going to be this TV just like there
was radio and when it comes the Buck Loner features are
going to be worth their weight in solid platinum.' But he
paid me no mind and . . . But that's not what we were
talking about. No. It was about the kids, yes." He
frowned. "Now they are good kids who for the most
part come from underprivileged homes across the length
and breadth of this country, and they hitchhike to sunny
California in order that they might be stars, like me.
They get jobs here and there to support themselves while
they study at the Academy where we do our darnedest
to bring out the creative potential of each and every
one . . ."

"Can the brochure, daddy," I said, surprising myself

by the Fifties jargon that so amused Myron but rather
repelled me. "You're in business to make money, and you
do."

He looked genuinely hurt. "Well now, honey, of
course I am making money or I should say *eking* out
an existence, real estate taxes being what they are in this
high-type residential area . . ." Noticing the scorn in
my face (and realizing that I am on to his conning), he
quickly got away from the ticklish subject of our mutual
property.

"Anyway, I genuinely want to see these boys and girls
happy because — you may laugh and probably will — I
believe in Love and I try to create that sort of atmos-
phere here where they are as much as possible screened
from the harshness of the world, which they get quite
enough of working as waitresses in drive-ins and so on,
not to mention the unhappy often broken homes they
come from. I try to give them the glamour and excitement of show business, of fame, of stardom without the
pain of failure, the terrible ordeal of real-life show business where so many hearts are broken every day, needlessly, but that's the way it goes. Here at least they are
able to perform on our closed-circuit TV and then read
the reviews in our school paper which are always good
and constructive. They can cut discs which are played
on our Muzak-type system. They have special courses in
how to give interviews to the press which they can then
read in the school magazine. In fact, until it was recently
discontinued, our late-night closed-circuit TV talk show
was as good as NBC's, with our stars being interviewed
by a fellow student, himself a star on the order of

Johnny Carson. So with all those things, for a time, within these walls, more than a thousand young men and women with stars in their eyes are happy."

No doubt about it, he was most effective. When he spoke of hearts needlessly broken (the sort of phrase Myron would have hooted at), I confess tears came to my eyes. For he was paraphrasing Betty Hutton after one of her many failures on television. She never had any luck, that girl. Possibly because she does not realize that she is a true goddess, as a result of all those pictures she made at Paramount during the Forties; films in which she was the demonic clown, the drum majorette of Olympus or, as Parker Tyler puts it with his usual wisdom: "The Hutton comedienne is a persuasive hieroglyph that symbolizes something deeply ingrained in modern morality: the commoner man's subconscious impulse, when a girl evades or refuses a kiss, to knock her out, take it, and have done."

Never was Tyler more on the mark than when he analyzed Hutton's "epileptico-mimetic pantomime," in which he saw straight through the strenuous clowning to the hard fact that American women are eager for men to rape them and vice versa; and that in every American there is a Boston Strangler longing to break a neck during orgasm. Ours is a violent race.

Buck and I agreed to disagree. But though he is a fool, he is also a man of formidable character and persuasiveness and thus a dangerous antagonist. It will require all my genius to destroy him . . . and destroy him I must, for not only has he cheated me of Myron's proper inheritance, he represents all that I detest in the post-Forties culture: a permissive slovenliness of mind and art. It is all like, like, like . . . "like help," as the Californian said when he was drowning. They all use "like" in a way that sets my teeth on edge. Not that I am strict as a grammarian. I realize that a certain looseness of style is necessary to create that impression of spontaneity and immediacy which is the peculiar task of post-Gutenberg prose, if there is to be such a thing. But I do object to "like" because of its mindless vagueness. "What time is it, Rusty?"

"Like three o'clock, Miss Myra," he said, after looking at his watch. He knew the *exact* time but preferred to be approximate. Well, I shall teach him to tell time among other things.

BUCK LONER REPORTS —
Recording Disc No. 715 —
5 February

        Flagler and Flagler dont seem to be getting much of anywhere with the case they say that Gertrudes will is in order leaving her share of the property to Myron and Myrons will though not made by a lawyer was duly witnessed and will stand up in court leaving everything to his wife Myra so half the property is hers according to law which strikes me as perfect injustice since if it wasnt for me there wouldnt be hardly any value at all to this land even though it is Westwood the lawyers sug gest I settle with her for the current going price of these acres in Westwood for land which would be in the neighborhood of two hundred thousand bucks which I am not about to pay also I got a hunch she is out for even bigger game for she has lately taken to making little jokes about what a swell team we make running the Academy I hate that woman and wish to God there was some way to get her out of my hair once and for all Flagler and Flagler are now checking up to make sure she was really married to that fag nephew thats our only hope at this point proving she wasnt married or something meanwhile I cozy her along best I can period paragraph the tak ing of drugs is frowned upon by this institution not only is it illegal and injurious to the health but it has been known to be harmful to the performances of those performing while under the influence some thing along those lines I must write up for the paper before the vice squad gets on my ass any more than they are now its crazy with people murdering each other from one end of L A to the other all our local storm troopers can think of is kids smoking pot which does them a lot less harm than liquor well it is a nutty world and that is for sure period para graph dont forget to tell Hilda to send me the new French Canadian masseuse on Monday they say she gives a super around the world and also knows about massage remember to pick up chutney for Bobbie Dean whos cooking curry tonight

13

I have locked the bathroom door. Several people have tried to get in, including Rusty, but I call out to them, "Use the other john," and they go away, doubtless thinking that I am in here with a man when actually I am simply trying to get away from the party.

I feel very odd. I just smoked one entire marijuana cigarette, something I have never done before. In the old days Myron and I used occasionally to take a drag on someone else's joint but never an entire stick. I always thought that drugs had no effect on me but apparently I was wrong.

I feel like crying. The ring around the bathtub, no, the two rings, one light, one dark, his and hers, depress me. What am I doing? I, Myra Breckinridge, Woman, as I proceed in my long trailing robes across the desert. Suddenly I catch sight of my lover, a priest who has given up hope of Heaven for my body. I throw out my arms and run toward him across the silvery sands. . . .

I can hardly write. My eyes don't focus properly but I must put down all my impressions exactly for they are extraordinarily intense and important. The door of perception has swung open at last and now I know that what I always suspected was true is true, that time is space made fluid, that these miniskirts are too short for me; that time is a knee made fluid. That is hell.

14

A terrible hangover, the result of mixing gin and marijuana, though pot is supposed not to leave one with any ill effect, unless of course that is simply a legend cultivated by drug addicts. I am in my office, trying to prepare for the first class of the day. Only with the greatest effort am I able to write these lines. My hands tremble. I feel quite ill.

The party was given by one of the students in the Music Department, Clem or Clint something or other. I had never seen him before but yesterday morning Gloria Gordon (who is in my Empathy I class) told me that he gave marvelous "far-out" parties and that I would be welcome to come last night as he, Clem or Clint, had admired me from a distance.

So Laura came to Petrarch's party, to put it stylishly, and got stoned out of her head. It was too humiliating and yet during those moments when I lay in that empty bathtub with the two rings, staring up at the single electric light bulb, I did have the sense that I was at one with all creation. The notes I made under the influence do not *begin* to record what I was actually feeling, largely because I was forced to break them off when a kind of paralysis set in. Apparently I was not able to move or speak until shortly before dawn when Clem or Clint and Gloria broke the lock on the bathroom door and rescued me from my gaudy reveries.

Fortunately, they took it all as a huge joke, but I am still humiliated at having got myself in such a situation, without dignity and finally without revelation, for in the light of day I find it difficult to believe in cosmic consciousness. In fact, this terrible hangover seems to me proof that the celebrated insights of the mystics are physiological, the result of a drastic reduction of sugar in the blood that goes to the brain. *My* brain, deprived of sugar for some hours last night, now feels as if it were full of an expanding fluid on the verge of seeking desperate egress through the top of a papier-mâché skull.

I did find the party interesting, at least in its early stages. Of those present, I was one of the oldest, which did nothing for my sense of security so laboriously achieved in those long sessions with Dr. Montag. But I was a good sport, laughing and chatting and, all in all, behaving not as a teacher but as just plain Myra Breckinridge, a beautiful woman not yet thirty. As a result, several of the young men showed a sexual interest in me but though I teased them and played the flirt, I did not allow any intimacies to occur or even indicate that they might be welcomed at some future time. I preferred to be Greer Garson, a gracious lady whose compassionate breasts were more suited to be last pillow for a dying youth than as baubles for the coarse hands of some horny boy.

But sex does not appear to be the hangup with this crowd. They wear buttons which, among other things, accuse the Governor of California of being a Lesbian, the President of being God, and Frodo (a character in a fairy tale by Tolkien) of actually existing. This is all a bit fey for my taste. But one must be open to every experience and the young, in a sense, lead us since there are now more of them than there are of us. But they are peculiar creatures, particularly to one brought up within the context of the Forties. They are quite relaxed about sex; not only do they have affairs with one another, they also attend orgies in a most matter-of-fact way, so unlike my generation with its belief in the highly concentrated sort of love that Leslie Howard felt for Ingrid Bergman in *Intermezzo.* Yet despite all this athleticism, their *true* interests seem to be, in some odd way, outside sex. They like to sit for long periods doing nothing at all, just listening to music or to what they regard as music. They are essentially passive; hence the popularity of pot.

Of course, my generation (chronologically, not spiritually) began all this. We of the Fifties saw the beginning of Zen as a popular force. Certainly our Beats were nothing if not passive in their attitude to life and experience. They were always departing, never arriving. Neither Myron nor I shared their pleasures or attitudes for we were, despite our youth, a throwback to the Forties, to the last moment in human history when it was possible to possess a total commitment to something outside oneself. I mean of course the war and the necessary elimination of Hitler, Mussolini and Tojo. And I do not exaggerate when I declare that I would give ten years of my life if I could step back in time for just one hour and visit the Stage Door Canteen in Hollywood, exactly the way that Dane Clarke did in the movie of the same name, and like him, meet all the great stars at their peak and perhaps even, like Dane's buddy Bob Hutton, have a romance with Joan Leslie, a star I fell hopelessly in love with while watching *Sergeant York*. But where is Joan now? Where are all those beautiful years of war and sacrifice and Pandro S. Berman films? None of this will ever come again, except in gray cloudy miniatures on the Late Show, and soon, I pray, in the sinewy prose of Myra Breckinridge as she reworks and completes her late husband's certain-to-be masterpiece *Parker Tyler and the Films of the Forties*.

But what will the current generation think of my efforts? That is the question. I find that any reference to the stars of the Forties bores them. "Who was Gary Cooper?" asked one young thing last night; to which another girl answered, "The one with the big ears," thinking he was Clark Gable! But they all find Humphrey Bogart fascinating and he may yet prove to be my bridge to them.

Conversation from last night.

"Like experience isn't everything, Myra. I mean like you also got to have *it* deep down inside you."

"But what is *it*?"

"What's deep down inside you, that's what *it* is. What you are."

"But isn't what you are what experience makes you?"

"No, it's like what you feel . . ."

Like. Like. Like! The babble on this subculture is drowning me! Although my companion was a lanky youth of the sort I am partial to, I simply shut him out and watched the group that was dancing in the center of the room, a dozen boys and girls gyrating without touching one another, each in his or her private world . . . which is the key to the game of the moment: don't touch me and I won't touch you. While the operative word is "Cool." Like fun? Like crazy!

Of the dancers, Rusty Godowsky was easily the most exciting and certainly the most attractive, in his faded chinos and checked shirt, whose top two buttons were missing, revealing a smooth muscular neck at whose base, just below the hollows of the collarbone, tendrils of bronze hair curl, looking as if they would be silky to the touch, unlike the usual male Brillo. Soon I shall know for certain their texture. Poor Mary-Ann.

"He does dance well, doesn't he?" Mary-Ann sat down in the place which the metaphysician had vacated, without, I fear, my noticing his departure. Obviously she had seen me watching Rusty. She is not entirely stupid.

"I was studying him for posture." I sounded colder than I intended, but she had taken me by surprise and I dislike it when people observe me without my knowledge. "I will say he moves very well when he dances," I added with a degree of warmth which encouraged her to smile shyly.

"That's being an athlete. It's just when he walks he sort of lumbers."

"Well, we'll soon take care of that," I said briskly, and indeed I shall, poor bastard.

Mary-Ann chattered away, unaware of my designs. "We've been talking about maybe getting married in June after we finish the course—that is, if we can both get work. Of course I can always pick up a little money modeling. I'm not really crazy about a career, you know. Fact, it's just to be with Rusty that I'm taking this music course, to keep an eye on him. With all these pretty girls around and wild for him, I can't take any chances."

"You make a charming couple." I noticed again how extraordinarily attractive she is, with that fresh un-clouded complexion I so love—and envy, for the texture of the skin of my face is not all that Helena Rubinstein would desire. In my day I have been too much a sun-worshipper and the skin must pay a price for the spirit's refreshment, and I was certainly refreshed by those long sunny afternoons at Jones Beach and amongst the Far Rockaways.

Rusty's back was to us now and I could not take my eyes off his somewhat square yet small buttocks as they made a slow grinding motion in response to the beat of an electric guitar. Though I tried to visualize what they must look like without the protective covering of cloth, I failed to come up with a satisfactory mental image. Happily, I shall soon know everything!

" 'Course we're both broke. I get a little something from the family in Winnipeg but poor Rusty's only got this uncle and aunt in Detroit who don't like him because he was kind of wild when he was a kid . . ."

"So wild that he was busted for stealing a car." The day that I first noticed Rusty in class, I went straight to Buck's office where dossiers on each student are kept.

They are surprisingly thorough. Rusty's three-year sus-
pended sentence was duly noted, as well as the cogent
fact that should he ever again run afoul of the law he can
be sent up for a maximum of twenty years.

Mary-Ann looked frightened. "I didn't know anybody knew about that."

"Just Uncle Buck and I." I patted her hand. "Don't
worry, neither of us is going to tell."

"He's completely changed since those days, he really
is. Why, in those days he used to play around with a lot
of girls. You should have seen all the photographs he
used to have! But after he met me he stopped all that and
now he isn't interested in anything except working hard
and being a star, which I'm sure he's going to be."

"He's certainly no worse than the rest of them on television." I was perfectly honest with her. "Of course he
can hardly talk but neither can they."

"Oh, but he talks awfully well. It's just he has some
trouble with *speaking* lines but that takes lots of practice.
Anyway what is important is that he comes over so *real*,
and of course so sexy. You should have seen him on the
closed-circuit TV last spring when he played the part of
this crazy gunman. Oh, he was *something!*"

It was at that point that I was given marijuana by Clem
or Clint, and the rest of the evening took on a religious
tone.

15

Feeling somewhat better, I gave a great deal to my Empathy II class, and though I am now exhausted, I have at least gotten over my hangover.

A letter from Dr. Montag cheered me up. He warns against depressions of the sort I have been prone to since Myron's death and so he proposes, rather obviously, that in lieu of analysis I must keep busy. Little does he dream just how busy I am! Between my plot to entrap Rusty and my efforts to obtain my rightful share of the Academy, I have hardly a moment to devote to my life's real work, completing Myron's book. Fortunately the insights gained during my visit to MGM are bound to add immeasurably to Myron's text. Meanwhile, I have had a marvelous idea for a piece on Pandro S. Berman which *Cahiers du Cinema* ought to eat up. After all, with the exception of Orson Welles and Samuel Fuller, Berman is the most important film-maker of the Forties.

16

I spoke sharply to Rusty in Posture today. He shows no sign of improvement and I'm afraid I was brutal. "You simply cannot walk straight." I imitated his slouching walk which is, in its way, extremely sensual but hardly suitable for the screen.

He looked very angry and muttered something under his breath that I could not hear but assumed was uncomplimentary. Mary-Ann looked more than ever disturbed as she begged me with her eyes to desist.

"I will see you after class, Godowsky." I was abrupt. "Things cannot go on as they are," I added ominously.

I then gave the class a series of exercises in how to sit down, something that did not come easily to any of them. All the while observing, out of the corner of my eye, Rusty's sullen face. My plot is working very nicely.

After class, Rusty came to my office and sat on the straight chair beside the desk, listing to one side, legs wide apart. He was not in the least nervous. In fact, he

was downright defiant, even contemptuous of *me*, so secure did he think himself in his masculine superiority.

As usual, he wore a sport shirt with two missing buttons. Today, however, a T-shirt hid the chest from view.
Faded blue jeans and desert boots completed the cos-
tume, and — as I have already noted — it is costumes that
the young men now wear as they act out their simple-
minded roles, hopefully constructing a fantasy world in
order to avoid confronting the fact that to be a man in a
society of machines is to be an expendable, soft auxiliary
to what is useful and hard. Today there is nothing left
for the old-fashioned male to do, no ritual testing of his
manhood through initiation or personal contest, no physical struggle to survive or mate. Nothing is left him but
to put on clothes reminiscent of a different time; only in
travesty can he act out the classic hero who was a law
unto himself, moving at ease through a landscape filled
with admiring women. Mercifully, that age is finished.
Marlon Brando was the last of the traditional heroes and,
significantly, even he was invariably beaten up in the last
reel, victim of a society that has no place for the ancient
ideal of manhood. Since Brando, there has been nothing
except the epicene O'Toole, the distracted Mastroianni,
and the cheerfully incompetent Belmondo. The roof has
fallen in on the male and we now live at the dawn of the
age of Woman Triumphant, of Myra Breckinridge!

I began pleasantly, disarmingly. "Not long ago Mary-
Ann told me that I have a tendency to pick on you,
Rusty . . ."

"You sure do . . ."

"Don't interrupt, please." I was stern but pleasant, like

Eve Arden. "If I have, it's because I'm trying to help
you. I think you have great *potential* talent. How great I
can't decide just yet, but unless you learn to walk properly there's not a chance in this world of your ever being
a major star."

The reference to his talent pleased him; the prophecy
alarmed him. "Hell, Miss Myra, I don't walk that bad."

"I'm afraid you do. And look at the way you're leaning to one side right now. You look like you're about to
fall out of the chair."

He straightened up and crossed his legs. "That better?" The hint of a sneer in his voice excited me. He must
be built up in order that his fall be the more terrible.

"Yes. Now I realize that you have a physical problem.
Mary-Ann told me about your back."

"I broke four ribs and even so finished the last half."
He was inordinately proud; no doubt about it, a confident young man.

"Very admirable. Now I want you to stand up and
walk first toward the door and then back here to me."

I could hear him murmur "Oh, shit" under his breath
as he lumbered to his feet. Slowly he walked, or rather
slouched, to the door and then returned and stood defi-
antly in front of me, thumbs hooked in his belt. I noted
for the first time how large and strong his hands are, hairless with unusually long thumbs.

"O.K.?" he asked.

"*Not* O.K." I studied him a moment. He was so close
to me that my eyes were on a level with his belt buckle.
"Now, Rusty, I noticed the other night that your problem seems to go away when you dance. So, just as an

exercise, I want you to do one of those stationary dances
— I don't know what they're called. You know, like the
one you were doing at the party."

"Dance? Here? Now?" He looked puzzled. "But
there's no music."

"To be precise there never is *music* with those dances,
just electronic noise. Nothing compared to the *big* sound
of Glenn Miller. Anyway, all you need is a beat. You can
keep time by snapping your fingers."

"I feel silly." He scowled and looked suddenly dangerous, but I knew what I was about.

"Go ahead. We haven't got all day. Start." I snapped
my fingers. Halfheartedly he did the same and slowly
began to gyrate his hips. I found the effect almost un-
bearably erotic. To have him all to myself, just three feet
away, his pelvis revolving sexily. For some minutes he
continued to gyrate, the snapping of fingers growing less
and less precise as his hands grew sweaty. I then in-
structed him to turn around so that I could observe him
from the rear. He did as he was told. Waves of lust made
me dizzy as those strong deep buttocks slowly revolved.
Have they ever been violated? I can hardly bear the sus-
pense.

Finally, I told him he could stop. He did so, with obvious relief. When he turned back to me, I noticed the
curved upper lip was beaded with perspiration. In his
dense masculine way, he too had felt the tension and perhaps suspected, instinctively, its origin and so knew fear.
"I can't dance so good without music," he mumbled, as if
obscurely ashamed of the display he had been forced to
make of himself.

"You did very well." I was brisk, even encouraging. "I think I may have a solution to our problem. All you need is something to remind you to stand straight. Where were the ribs broken?"

He touched his left side, below the heart. "Four was busted right here which is why I'm kind of pulled over to this side."

"Let me see."

At first he seemed not to understand the question. "Like this," he said, indicating the way in which he was listing to port.

"No. No." I was brusque. "Let me *see* your back. Take your shirt off."

He was startled. "But there's nothing to see. . . . I mean the ribs are all inside me that was broken."

"I know *where* the ribs are, Rusty." I was patient. "But I have to see the exact point where the muscle begins to pull you to one side."

There was no answer to this. He started to say something but decided not to. Slowly he unfastened his belt and unhooked the top button of the blue jeans. Then he unbuttoned his shirt and took it off. The T-shirt was soaked at the armpits, the result of his strenuous impromptu dance and, perhaps (do I project?), of terror.

For the first time I saw his bare arms. The skin was very white (no one out here goes to the beach in January even though it is quite sunny), with biceps clearly marked though not overdeveloped; large veins ran the length of the forearms to the hands, always an excellent sign, and not unattractive since the veins were not blue but white, indicating skin of an unusual thickness, again a good sign. On the forearms coppery straight hairs grew. He paused as though not certain what to do next. I was helpful. "The T-shirt, too. I haven't got X-ray eyes."

Glumly he pulled the T-shirt over his head. I watched, fascinated by each revelation of his body. First the navel came into view, small and protruding. Just beneath it a line of dark slightly curly hairs disappeared inside the Jockey shorts which were now visible above the loosened belt. The shirt rose higher. About two inches above the navel, more hairs began (I had seen the topmost branches of this tree of life at the pot party, now I saw the narrow roots slowly widening as the tree made its way to his neck). When the chest was entirely bared, his face was momentarily hidden in the folds of the damp T-shirt and so I was able to study, unobserved, the small rose-brown breasts, at the moment concave and unaroused. Then the T-shirt was wadded up and dropped onto the floor.

Aware of my interested gaze, he blushed. Beginning at the base of the thick neck, the lovely color rose to the level of his eyes. Like so many male narcissists, he is, paradoxically, modest: he enjoys revealing himself but only on his own terms.

A remark about his appearance was obviously called for and I made it. "You seem in very good condition . . ."

"Well, I work out some, not like I ought to . . . used to . . ." He hooked long thumbs into his belt, causing the smooth pectorals to twitch ever so slightly, revealing the absence of any fat or loosening of skin.

"Now will you please face the wall, arms at your side,

with your palms pressed against the wall as hard as you can."

Without a word, he did as he was told. The back was as pleasing as the front (no hairs on the shoulder, unlike poor Myron, who was forced to remove his with electrolysis). The blue jeans had begun to sag and now hung several inches below the waistline, revealing frayed Jockey shorts. Aware that the trousers were slipping, he tried to pull them up with one hand but I put a stop to that. "Hands flat against the wall!" I ordered in a sharp voice that would not take no for an answer.

"But, Miss Myra . . ." and his voice was suddenly no longer deep but a boy's voice, plaintive and frightened: the young Lon McCallister.

"Do as I say!"

He muttered something that I could not hear and did as he was told. In the process, the blue jeans cleared the curve of his buttocks and now clung precariously to the upper thighs of which a good two inches were in plain view. It was a moment to cherish, to exult in, to give a life for. His embarrassment was palpable, charging the situation with true drama since from the very beginning it has been quite plain to me that *in no way do I interest him sexually*. Since he detests me, my ultimate victory is bound to be all the more glorious and significant.

I studied my captive for some moments (the spine did indeed make an S-like curve and the thick white trapezoidal ligament was twisted to one side). Of greater interest to me, however, were the Jockey shorts and what they contained. But now I knew that I would have to proceed with some delicacy. I crossed to where he stood.

I was so close to him that I could smell the horselike odor men exude when they are either frightened or in a state of rut. In this case it was fright.

Delicately I ran my hand down his spine. He shuddered at my touch but said nothing. Meanwhile I spoke to him calmly, easily, the way one does in order to soothe a nervous animal. "Yes, I can see the trouble now. It's right here, under the shoulder blade." I kneaded the warm smooth skin, and again he winced but said nothing while I continued to give my "analysis" of his condition. "Perhaps a brace in this area would help."

Now my hands were at the narrow waist. He was breathing hoarsely, arms pressed so hard against the wall that the triceps stood out like white snakes intertwined, ready to strike.

I felt something warm on the back of one hand: a drop of sweat from his left armpit. "But perhaps the trouble is lower down. Around the small of the back. Yes, of course! The lumbar region — that's just where it is!"

As I spoke, evenly, hypnotically, I gently inserted my thumbs beneath the worn elastic band of his shorts and before he was aware of what was happening, I had pulled them down to his knees. He gave a strangled cry, looked back over his shoulder at me, face scarlet, mouth open, but no words came. He started to pull away from me, then stopped, recalling that he was for all practical purposes nude. He clung now to the wall, the last protector of his modesty.

Meanwhile I continued to chat. "Yes, we can start the brace right here." I touched the end of the spine, a rather

protuberant bony tip set between the high curve of buttocks now revealed to me in all their splendor . . . and
splendor is the only word to describe them! Smooth,
white, hairless except just beneath the spinal tip where a
number of dark coppery hairs began, only to disappear
from view into the deep crack of buttocks so tightly
clenched that not even a crowbar could have pried them
apart.

Casually I ran my hand over the smooth slightly damp
cheeks. To the touch they were like highly polished marble warmed by the sun of some perfect Mediterranean
day. I even allowed my forefinger the indiscretion of fingering the coppery wires not only at the tip of the spine
but also the thicker growth at the back of his thighs. Like
so many young males, he has a relatively hairless torso
with heavily furred legs. Myron was the same. With age,
however, the legs lose much of this adolescent growth
while the torso's pelt grows heavier.

I had now gone almost as far as I could go with my
inspection. After all, I have not yet established total mastery. But I have made a good beginning: half of the mystery has now been revealed, the rest must wait for a more
propitious time. And so, after one last kneading of the
buttocks (I tried and failed to pull apart the cheeks), I
said, "That will do for now, Rusty. I think we've almost
got to the root of the problem."

He leaned rigidly, all of a piece, to one side and
grabbed the fallen trousers. Had he slightly squatted —
the normal thing to do in his position — I might have
caught a glimpse of the heart of the mystery from the

rear, an unflattering angle which, paradoxically, has always excited me, possibly because it is in some way involved with my passion for "backstage," for observing what is magic from the unusual, privileged angle. But he kept his legs as much together as possible, pulling on clothes with astonishing speed, the only lapse occurring when something in front was caught by the ascending shorts, causing him to grunt and fumble. But then all was in order and when he finally turned around, the belt buckle had been firmly fastened. He was satisfyingly pale and alarmed-looking.

I was all business. "I think this has been a very useful session — yes, you can put on your shirt." His hands trembled as he buttoned his shirt. "I'll have a chat with the chiropractor Uncle Buck uses" (the "Uncle Buck" always works wonders at the Academy) "and we'll see what he can do for you."

"Yes, Miss Myra." The voice was almost inaudible. Nervously, he mopped his face with a handkerchief.

"It is stuffy in here, isn't it? I always turn the airconditioning off. It's bad for my sinus. Well, I don't want to keep you another minute from Mary-Ann. What a wonderful girl! I hope you realize how lucky you are."

"Oh, yes, Miss Myra, I sure do," he gabbled. Then, with the assurance that I had only his interest at heart, I showed him out of the room. It was, in many ways, the most exciting *sensual* moment of my life — so far. But the best is yet to come, for I mean to prove once and for all to Dr. Montag that it is possible to work out in life *all* one's fantasies, and so become entirely whole.

No sooner was Rusty out the door than I noticed he

had left his T-shirt behind. I buried my face in its warm sweaty folds, a most agreeable surrogate for skin. The odor was somewhat sharp at the armpits but by no means unpleasant since fresh sweat is the greatest of aphrodisiacs as well as nature's own lubricant.

BUCK LONER REPORTS —
Recording Disc No. 721 —
18 February
　　　　　Dont know when I have ever come
across a woman as awful as Myra Breckinridge she
is wreaking total havoc with the program telling the
students they have no talent and no chance of star
dom which is downright mean not to mention bad
for business so I had a talk with her in the back of
the auditorium where she was holding her Empathy
class which for reasons not clear to me is double
the size of any of the other classes the kids are fas
cinated by her because of what she says and she is
a sharptongued bitch no doubt of that theres seldom
a class of hers where somebody dont run out crying
to beat the band but they come back for more which
is downright unhealthy as I told her in no uncertain
terms you are undermining all of our work here at
the Academy which is to build up capital c confi
dence exclamation point paragraph well she just
gave me that high and mighty stare of hers and said

you think lying to people is good for them you think telling somebody whos got cancer that he is all right and doesnt need an operation is the right thing to do of course not I said but if he has had the operation and is a terminal case I think you must keep him as happy as possible and in a good frame of mind under the circumstances well she said in a voice so loud that the students on the stage who were pretending to be billboards could hear her at least you admit that these cretins are terminal cases and that its curtains for the lot of them no it is not I said want ing to crack her one against the side of her head just to take that smirk off of her face no they are carefully selected as possible candidates for future stardom every last one of them well then she inter rupts with a single swear word delivered in a hiss that I swear sent shivers down my spine like some mean old rattler out there in the sagebrush just wait ing to sink his fangs into your leg well I was not about to be put down in my own Academy and so I said getting real tough you don't talk to me that way and get away with it you consider yourself warned or else Ill have you out of here so fast you wont know what hit you to which she just smiled prettily and cocked her pretty head at me and said ever so sweet you just try it you motherfucker and Ill take this whole place away from you lock stock and Em pathy class well I dont think no woman has ever spoke to me like that certainly no man would dare for fear of getting hisself beat to a pulp all I could say then was well you watch your step thats all and as for taking this place away from me I need to know a whole lot more about you than I do why I dont even know whether you was ever really mar ried to that fag Myron well I suppose I did go too far on that one for she hauled off and let me have it

right in the kisser and I saw stars because this wasnt
no girls slap no sir it was a goddam fist with what
felt like a roll of quarters in it I nearly fell over it was
such a jolt and the noise mustve been like a pistol
going off for the kids all stopped pretending to be
billboards and stared at us like we was putting on
a show which is the way she handled it for cool as
can be she said to the kids I quote now that is the
classic stage slap delivered in such a way that
though the person being slapped really seems to be
hit hard he isnt its all fake later Ill show you how
its done its a trick first used on stage by Miss Patricia
Collinge in The Little Foxes so thank you Uncle
Buck for the demonstration unquote and with that
the bitch went back to teaching her class and I come
straight back here to the office and canceled my ap
pointment for massage I am too shook up and then
phoned to Flagler and Flagler to ask if theres any
report on her from the detective in New York they
say the only thing theyve so far found is that Myron
really was a fag quite well known in what they call
the underground movie set and its thought he killed
hisself probably because of Myra about who they
cant find out anything except there is no record of
her marrying him in New York New Jersey or Con
necticut they are meanwhile going to check the
other forty-seven states it would be the happiest day
of my life if I can find out she really wasn't married
to him and put her in the damned hoosegow for
fraud on the other hand the three wills are all in
order worse luck for me so everything depends now
on that marriage license dont forget Bobbie Deans
yoghurt with prune whip

17

I am sitting in a booth at Schwab's drugstore in Hollywood where the young Lana Turner was discovered by an agent. Of course the present Schwab's does not in the least resemble the Schwab's of thirty years ago. Today's drugstore consists of two large rooms. The one where I am sitting contains booths while the other is occupied by drugstore, soda fountain and a large display of magazines and paperback books where out-of-work actors and actresses can be seen at any time of day or night furtively reading *Silver Screen*, or searching feverishly through the pages of novels looking for lurid passages whose crude imagery can be calculated to enliven sexual bouts with "loved ones" or, as one hippie said to another after sex, "I'll tell you who I was thinking of if you'll tell me who you were thinking of."

It is curious how often the male (and sometimes the female) needs to think of those not present in the act. Even with Myron, I was always imagining someone else, a boy glimpsed at Jones Beach or a man observed briefly at the wheel of a truck or sometimes (yes, I may as well confess it) a slender blonde girl that used to live in the brownstone next door when we lived at the corner of 11th Street and Ninth Avenue. She studied at the Art Students League and though I never once spoke to her, I was constantly aware of her and learned a good deal about her from the owner of the Ninth Avenue Delicatessen where each of us had an account, ours too seldom paid on time.

Fortunately, I am no longer susceptible to the charm of the female body. Not that a straightforward invitation from the young Lana Turner or the young Ava Gardner might not, as they say out here, "turn me on," but luckily for me there is no longer a young Lana Turner or Ava Gardner and so my lust has taken a different and quite spectacular form since Myron's death.

Rusty has been avoiding me ever since the day of his humiliation. He has even taken to cutting Posture class, which is a serious matter. This morning as I was on my way to Empathy II (held in the auditorium because of the students' desire to be taught by me: the other teachers are mad with envy!), I bumped into Rusty — literally collided with him at the turning of a corridor. I dropped my briefcase, which he swiftly retrieved.

"I'm sorry, Miss Myra." He handed me the briefcase at arm's length as though it contained a ticking bomb.

"You really should watch where you're going." I was severe and he gulped like Gary Cooper, his attractiveness greatly enhanced by a total inability to look me in the eye.

"You've missed two Posture classes in a row. That's very serious, Rusty. Very, very serious. You know how Uncle Buck dislikes that, and how it is bound to count against your final grade."

"But I been real busy, Miss Myra. Working, see . . ."

"The garage?"

"No, with these friends, helping to start this business. Anyway, next week I'll be back in class and that's for sure, Miss Myra." He looked at me with such frightened sincerity that it was all I could do to keep my hands off him right then and there. Gone was the easy masculine arrogance that had characterized him in our early relations. Now he was jittery and profoundly hostile, and all because of *me!* Though the corridor was airconditioned to a polar temperature (like so many fat men Buck suffers from heat), a bead of sweat appearing at the tip of one sideburn reminded me to say, "I still have the T-shirt you left in my office."

Bright red at this reference to his humiliation, he said that he was sorry to be so forgetful and that, if it was all right, he would come around sometime and retrieve the garment. Then the bell rang for class and we parted. I watched him a moment as he ran down the corridor, the buttocks that once I had beheld in all their innocent naked glory covered now by thick corduroy. Soon I shall have occasion to examine them again, at leisure, as his education continues, impelling each of us inexorably toward the last degree.

The class went well until Buck decided to look in. I tolerated his presence. But then when he became critical of me I was forced to take a stern line with him. In fact,

after he made a direct challenge to my authority, I struck
him. All in all, it was a most satisfying thing to do and it
will be some time before that keg of lard dares to cross
me again.

Afterwards, in the faculty room (wall-to-wall cham-
pagne-beige carpeting, piped-in music, and a color television set), two of my colleagues joined me for coffee
from the mechanical dispenser. Apparently "everyone"
has heard that there was some sort of contretemps between me and the president of the Academy. But I assured them that Uncle Buck and I could never quarrel
about anything. "Oh, perhaps a disagreement or two
about how far one should go in telling the students
whether or not they really do have talent."

Unfortunately both my colleagues share the Buck
Loner philosophy. One of them is a Negro queen named
Irving Amadeus. A recent convert to the Bahai religion,
he lives entirely on organic foods raised in a series of pots
in the backyard of a large house at Van Nuys which he
shares with a number of fellow cultists. There are, incidentally, nine Negro teachers but only seven Negro students. Though I suspect that Buck dislikes our dusky
cousins, he has done his best to integrate the school at the
teaching level, leaning over backwards to give work to
almost any show-biz-type Negro who comes his way
(the Stepin Fetchit Lecture Series, however, fell
through at the last moment, due to a contractual snag).
But at the student level, integration has not been easy. A
vocal minority are prejudiced, possibly because many
young white males fear the Negro cock. Time and again
I have observed white youths inadvertently clench their

buttocks at the approach of a black man, as though fear-
ful of anal penetration, not realizing that the legend of
Negro size is just that — legend. The dozen or so jungle
bunnies I have trafficked with were perfectly ordinary in
that department . . . in fact, two were hung like chip-
munks (Myron, incidentally, was larger than any of
them, a fact which, paradoxically, caused him not joy
but despair). The physiological origin of the myth was
once explained to me by Dr. Montag. Apparently the
Negro penis limp is almost the same size as it is when
erect, a phenomenon which, though it causes consternation in a shower room, brings no added joy to the bedroom. Nevertheless, uneasy white males still continue to
tighten their rosy sphincters at the approach of spooks.

In defense of the Buck Loner philosophy, Irving
Amadeus (he pretends to have been Jewish before his
conversion to Bahai) spoke of love. "It is necessary to
have love for all things, particularly those young people
entrusted to our care."

"Love," I said, "ought never to exclude truth."

"But love does not wound." He continued for some
time in this vein. Fortunately Miss Cluff, the other
teacher, has no interest in love, at least of the caritas sort.
She is lean and profoundly Lesbian, forever proposing
that we go to drive-in movies together in her secondhand
Oldsmobile. Temporarily she is teaching the Bell Telephone Hour Course in Song in order to make enough
money to pay for a concert debut in New York.

"Nonsense!" she said to Bahai, cutting him short. "We
must wound if we are to create artists. I myself am the
result of an uncle whom I hated, a teacher of piano who

forced me at the age of nine to practice seven, eight, ten hours a day, striking my fingers with a stick whenever I got a note wrong. This was in Oregon." We all recognized the plot of *The Seventh Veil* and so were able to ask the right questions in order to help her complete the fantasy whose denouement was that, in spite of everything, she had come through, become an artist, after the obligatory nervous breakdown, et cetera, and she owed it all to her uncle who had been cruel but *cared*.

I found this conversation pleasing, for I am always happy when people resort to the storehouse of movie myth in order to create for themselves attractive personas. I was not prepared, however, for her next observation. "There is really only one talented student in any of my classes and that is a girl called Mary-Ann Pringle."

I sat up, almost spilling the dregs of my coffee. *Had I missed a trick?* "But I know the girl. I have her in Posture. She is a complete nothing."

"Except," said Black Beauty, "for her connection with Rusty Godowsky. I have him in Atavistic Rhythm, and I am here to tell you that that ofay boy has really got sex appeal in spades!" (All in all, not a happy figure of speech, I thought.)

"I know *what* he's got," I said too quickly, and not quite accurately.

"Then you know he is absolutely total man, or, as we in Bahai believe . . ."

"What," I turned to Miss Cluff, drowning out Mother Africa, "is so talented about Mary-Ann Pringle?"

"Her *voice!* It is the pure, the white *bel canto*. Untrained, of course, like a smudged diamond, but a jewel

no less. She could be a star of the same magnitude
as . . ."

"Kathryn Grayson?"

Miss Cluff is too young to know from experience the
Forties and too self-absorbed to attend films seriously.
For her the movies are simply a pretext for getting girls
onto the back seat of her secondhand Oldsmobile. "She
could . . . she *must* sing opera."

But Darkness at Noon saw, perhaps rightly, another
fate for Mary-Ann. "As long as that young man wants
her she won't have a career. And from what I've seen of
him these last two years, he shows no sign of losing interest. Every girl in Atavistic Rhythm has made a play for
Rusty, and no dice."

Miss Cluff looked grim. "Women's rights are never
won! Never! To think that a girl of her talent is prepared to waste her life — and genius — on a hulk, an oaf,
a thing, a man!"

"A mighty *cute* thing," giggled Heart of Darkness,
but then recalled himself to add, more seriously, "and talented, too, possessing a natural animal magnetism, and of
course highly photogenic as we all of us saw last spring,
before Myra joined us, when he acted in a Rod Serling
classic on the closed-circuit TV . . ."

Although I usually collect every comment testifying
to Rusty's male attractiveness, adding bit by bit to the
vivid mosaic that is Rusty the Man (soon to be shattered
by me into a million fragments, that I may then rearrange
him along other and more meaningful lines), I suddenly
found myself morbidly eager to hear about Mary-Ann.
Miss Cluff, eager to tell, told. And I believed her.

Though mad as a hatter, Miss Cluff is every bit as tough-minded about the arts as I am. And so I am tempted to believe her when she tells me that *Mary-Ann has star quality*.

The columnist Sidney Skolsky has just entered the main part of the drugstore. Everyone stares at him. As well they might! With Louella and Hedda gone, he is Mr. Movies. They say his office is upstairs.

18

I am home now. The blinds are raised and I have been staring for some minutes at the bespangled ten-times-life-size girl as she slowly turns in front of the Château Marmont. For me she is Hollywood, and mesmerizing.

No further encounter with Rusty. He attended one Posture class but we did not speak and he was more than ever nervous and sullen in my presence. His T-shirt is still in my desk drawer, which now smells of him, a musky disturbing odor that makes me quite weak since, regretfully, I am not able to smell the original, for he keeps half a room's distance between us. I must soon make operative the second phase of my plan.

Meanwhile, to my surprise, Mary-Ann has been unusually friendly. When I told her yesterday that Miss Cluff thought her very talented, she was enormously pleased. "Miss Cluff *is* nice to say that. And I do like singing but, like Rusty says, there's only room for one star in any bed . . . I mean family." She stammered, blushing

deliciously at her error, which was no doubt a lovers'
joke.

"I'm sure that's what he *would* say. It's the usual male
view."

"But I like it. Honestly I do. I think the man's *got* to
be boss so a girl knows where she is."

"I'm afraid that's a slightly outmoded point of view." I
was careful, however, not to sound too sharp. "Particularly now when the relationship between the sexes is
changing so rapidly, and women are becoming aggressive
and men passive and . . ."

"Which I just hate!" Mary-Ann was unexpectedly
vehement. Good. The subject has occurred to her before. Excellent. "I hate these boys who just drift around,
taking pot and trips and not caring if — well, if it's a boy
or a girl they're with. It's just terrible the way so many
are now, and I guess that's why I'm so hung up on Rusty.
He's all man."

I thought with some amusement of "all man's" de-
fenseless bottom, quivering at my touch. I have the
power forever to alter her image of Rusty. But that is for
later. Now I must win her friendship, even love. The plan
requires it.

Although Dr. Montag and I write one another at least
once a week, I feel somewhat guilty for not having told
him what I am up to (these notes will be your introduc-
tion, dear Randolph). On the other hand, we do discuss
the one topic we most disagree on, the changing relationship between the sexes. Being Jewish as well as neo-
Freudian, he is not able to divest himself entirely of the

Law of Moses. For the Jew, the family is everything; if it had not been, that religion which they so cherish (but happily do not practice) would have long since ended and with it their baleful sense of identity. As a result, the Jew finds literally demoralizing the normal human sexual drive toward promiscuity. Also, the Old Testament injunction not to look upon the father's nakedness is the core to a puritanism which finds unbearable the thought that the male in himself might possess an intrinsic attractiveness, either aesthetically or sensually. In fact, they hate the male body and ritually tear the penis in order to remind the man so damaged that his sex is unlovely. It is, all in all, a religion even more dreadful than Christianity.

Dr. Montag, however, is a thoughtful man, aware of the damage done him as a child growing up in the household of a kosher butcher whose wife wanted their son to be a rabbi. But even then Randolph was a nonconformist; he chose to be a dentist, that last resort of the rabbi *manqué*. But dentistry soon palled (it was the tongue, not the teeth that interested him) and so he became a psychologist, and his book, *Sexual Role and/or Responsibility*, made a complete shambles of Karen Horney, among others.

Myron and I met Dr. Montag some years ago at a lecture Myron gave on "The Uterine Vision in the Films of the Forties" (this lecture is the basis for the chapter on Betty Hutton and Martha Raye in his Parker Tyler book). Needless to say, the lecture was sparsely attended. Myron was a nervous lecturer and his voice had a tendency to become shrill if he sensed any serious disagreement, and of course there was — is — always disagreement about his work as there is bound to be controversy about the work of any entirely original thinker.

On that famous night poor Myron was forced to shriek his way through the lecture in an effort to drown out the usual hecklers (this particular talk was given, like so many of his best performances, at the Blue Owl Grill on 132nd Street, a place where Happenings used to occur regularly before Happenings were known, and of course poets read). When the lecture was over and the booing had ceased, we were joined by a thickset man with blue jowls. "I am Randolph Spenser Montag," the man said, taking Myron's fragile hand into his own large one. "*Dr*. Montag," the man added but without unction or pride, merely a simple statement, "and I want you to know that you have broken new ground along lines similar to my own."

They talked until morning. I had never before known Myron to be so excited, so energized, so exalted as he was at that moment when he found for the first time in his life a masculine mind complementary to his own. This is not the place to review their joint achievements (as you know better than anyone, Randolph, and it is essentially for you and to you that I write in this notebook, a most liberating activity as well as an excellent way for me to tell you how much I admire you without any of the uneasiness caused by our usual face-to-face encounters, particularly those official ones when I am on the patient's couch and you are striding noisily about the room, wheezing and gasping from emphysema). That meeting in the Blue Owl was historic not only for the three of us but for the world, since many of the insights in *Sexual Role* as well as at least four chapters of Myron's Parker Tyler book can be said to have had their genesis in our knowing one another.

But now I am troubled by something in the letter just arrived. Referring to Myron with his usual fondness (do you deliberately want to set me off?), Dr. Montag remarked: "Myron's polymorphism (quite exceptional even by contemporary standards) was coupled with a desire to surrender entirely to the feminine side of his nature, symbolized by you. Yet I cannot help but believe that his masculinity was of great intensity, as you knew best, while the sadomasochistic proportion was quite evenly balanced. That is to say, he was as apt to beat up trade as be beaten up." This is not exactly correct. For all Dr. Montag's extraordinary sensitivity, he remains at heart a dentist of the most conventional kind. Myron's masculinity was, *at times*, intense, but the feminine aspects of his nature were the controlling ones, as I knew best. He wanted men to possess him rather than the other way around. He saw himself as a woman, made to suffer at the hands of some insensitive man. Needless to say, he found partners galore. When I think of the elaborate dinners he used to cook for merchant seamen with tattoos! The continual fussing about the house, so reminiscent of the female preparing to lay her egg! The humiliating position he would put himself in when some piece of trade spurned him because he was not able to lay on the requisite bread! Yet, paradoxically, Myron was physically quite strong despite the seeming fragility of his body and, properly aroused, he could beat up a man twice his

size; unfortunately, he took no more pleasure in this than
he did in the company of lovely girls. He was a tor-
mented creature, similar to Hart Crane, except that while
it was Crane's kick to blow those sailors he encountered
along the squalid waterfronts of that vivid never-to-be-
recaptured prewar world, Myron invariably took it from
behind. But though this was a source of great consolation
to Myron, Dr. Montag always felt, in his somewhat
naïve way, that Myron's obsession involved a certain
amount of gratuitous perversity, not to mention just
plain waste because Myron's own penis was exception-
ally large and much admired (it can be seen briefly in the
underground film *Lysol*). Dr. Montag never understood
that Myron's sexual integrity required him to withhold
that splendid penis from those who most needed it, thus
exerting power over them and what, finally, are human
relations but the desire in each of us to exercise absolute
power over others?

It is my view that the struggle to achieve power is the
underlying theme to all of Myron's work, even though
he never formulated it clearly. Certainly, *I* was never
able to do so until his death clarified so many things for
me. At the time I wanted to die, too. But then I entered
the next stage: mystical elation. I understood — or
thought I understood — *everything!* Myron's restless
cruising of bars was the result of a desire to draw into
himself, literally, that which men possess for quite another purpose. For him to be able to take from Woman
her rightful pleasure — not to mention the race's instrument of generation — became a means of exercising
power over *both* sexes and, yes, even over life itself!

That is why he was never drawn to homosexuals. In fact, once the man *wished* to penetrate him, Myron lost interest for then he himself would become the thing used, and so lose the power struggle. What excited him most was to find a heterosexual man down on his luck, preferably starving to death, and force him to commit an act repugnant to him but necessary if he was to be paid the money he needed for survival. At such moments, Myron confessed, he knew ecstasy: the forbidden was his! He had conquered Man, even though to the naïve observer it was Myron who *seemed* to be the one used. But he was almost always user, and that was his glory. Yet like all appetites, the one for power is insatiable. The more one obtains, the more one wants. In the end Myron could not, living, be what he wanted to be, an all-powerful user of men, and so he ended his life, leaving me to complete as best I can not only his masterpiece but the pattern he sought to make, with Dr. Montag's reluctant help.

Yet it is now plain to me that the good Doctor preferred Myron to me, and I cannot at times avoid a certain sense of hurt and rejection. Particularly when I realize that the only way the Doctor could be made happy would be if I were to marry and settle down. Dr. Montag still believes that each sex is intended to be half of a unit, like those monsters mentioned in Plato's *Symposium*. This is the Doctor's Mosaic side overwhelming common sense, not to mention the evidence of his senses. Admittedly *some* are best served when the struggle for power narrows to but one other person and the duel endures for a lifetime as mate attempts to destroy mate in that long wrangling for supremacy which is called mar-

riage. Most human beings, however, prefer the short
duet, lasting anywhere from five minutes with a stranger
to five months with a lover. Certainly the supreme moments occur only in those brief exchanges when each
party, absorbed by private fantasy, believes he is achieving mastery over the other. The sailor who stands against
a wall, looking down at the bobbing head of the gobbling
queen, regards himself as master of the situation; yet it is
the queen (does not that derisive epithet suggest primacy and dominion?) who has won the day, extracting
from the flesh of the sailor his posterity, the one element
in every man which is eternal and (a scientific fact) cel-
lularly resembles not at all the rest of the body. So to the
queen goes the ultimate elixir of victory, that which was
not meant for him but for the sailor's wife or girl or
simply Woman. Much of my interest in the capture of
Rusty is the thought that he is so entirely involved with
Mary-Ann. That gives value to what I mean to seize. If it
were freely offered, I would reject it. Fortunately he
hates me which excites me and so my triumph, when it
comes, will be all the sweeter.

BUCK LONER REPORTS —
Recording Disc No. 736 —
22 February
                    So decision has been made to pre
sent for the June jamboree a musical comedy based
on the life story of Elvis Presley who will I am sure
be present to see this show or better be since he isnt
doing all that well box office wise and could use the
publicity I dont know who can play the lead but we
got a lot of boys capable of singing like Elvis except
funnily enough I was surprised to see some objec
tions raised from some of the kids on the ground
that Elvis is old fashioned and another generation
like Bing Crosby well this made me feel old but I
said you got to have some traditional values and
respect the show business greats even when they are
over thirty years old the girl who will sing the girl
lead will be Mary Ann Pringle then there will be two
ninety minute closed circuit capital c color TV dra
mas from the old Playhouse 90 which again brings
a lot of criticism down on my head from the hippies

who have no respect for the classics of early tele
vision well they will learn better anyway we have
a lot of speaking parts in both plays and the western
lead will be Rusty Godowsky who is aimed for star
dom if he stays out of the clink write the Governor
another letter about the Ronald Reagan festival ex
plaining it was no joke but a serious offer for him
to M C the festival and gain good exposure period
good news at last from the lawyers about one Myra
Breckinridge who was never repeat never married
to my nephew in any one of the fifty United States
now Flagler and Flagler will fix her pretty wagon
and out she goes on her ass the way she is making
trouble around here is like some kind of God damned
plague of Egypt telling everybody how lousy they are
reminder to stop by Farmers Market and buy okra
Bobbie is cooking gumbo tonight

19

Clem Masters grows on one. At that first party when I became hopelessly stoned and passed out in the bathtub, I thought him the creep of the world. But since then I have got to know him and of all the students, he is the only one with something resembling a brain. He comes, needless to say, from the East (Buffalo, New York), and wants to be a singer but will probably settle for a career as songwriter. This morning, after Empathy, I met him in the corridor and he said, "Come on, baby, and let me play you something I just wrote."

"Wrote?" I asked. "Or stole from the Beatles like that last little number you recorded for Pop Tune IV . . ."

"You're a gas, Myra." He was not in the least distressed by my accusation of plagiarism. In fact, of all the students he alone seems not to fear me and since he interests me not at all sexually (he is weedy-looking with thick glasses and a black beard and never washes), I am able to enjoy his irreverence.

Clem took me into one of the music rooms where he promptly fell upon the piano and rushed through several loud syncopated numbers, bellowing banal lyrics at the top of his voice. When at last he stopped, I said the truth, as always, "It's just awful, Clem."

"You crazy mixed-up chick!" He laughed, he actually laughed at Myra Breckinridge! My first instinct was to slam shut the piano cover on his spidery fingers, breaking them all at once. But then I realized that his physical agony would do nothing for me, and so I laughed, too (a good sport like Carole Lombard), and said, "Why crazy? Why mixed-up?"

"Because what you heard is *music*, popular music and I am going to sell the whole mother score, piece by piece, to the Four Skins."

"What score? What skins?"

He looked at me pityingly. "The Four Skins are number four and number twenty-seven respectively in the January *Billboard*. So this score — which is for this mother life of Elvis Presley big Buck Loner has inflicted upon us — will make me some money."

"In that case, I think your songs are perfectly apt."

"I knew you had taste! Now listen, Myra, in some sick way you appeal to me. No, I really mean it. I dig you and I was thinking why don't we . . ."

"Clem." I was firm yet — how can I deny it? — flattered. After all, I am a woman. "I enjoy your company, you know that. You're the only student I can talk to but I could no more go to bed with you . . ."

"Baby, baby, baby . . ." He interrupted me impatiently. "Not with *me*, baby. I don't want to go to bed, the two of us. That's square. I mean a *party*, like maybe twenty cats . . ."

"*Twenty* men?" Not even my idlest daydreams of Myra Breckinridge, warrior queen, ever included a scene in which I was called upon to master twenty men at the same time. Might it not be too much, psychologically?

"Ten men and ten girls, you nit, or maybe seven of one and thirteen of the other or nine of one and eleven of the other. I mean who's *counting?* Want to make the scene?" Clem looked at me shrewdly through thick spectacles.

I was at a loss for words. On the one hand, the idea was definitely attractive. Myron sometimes enjoyed the company of four or five men at the same time but he did not believe in mixing the sexes. I of course do. Yet what pleasure, I calculated swiftly, would I extract from such a tableau? My little quirks can only be fulfilled with one man at a time.

I deliberately dithered, trying to make up my mind. "Oh, I don't think I should. Certainly not with people I know, not with the students."

"Not students, baby. I never let those cats in on anything if I can help it. No, you'll meet all five of the Four Skins and some crazy chicks . . . oh, it's your scene, I can tell . . ."

I knew that my hesitation had already betrayed my interest. "Perhaps I might just . . . *watch*, you know, and perhaps help out, in little ways . . ."

"All or nothing. No tourists allowed." He wrote an address on a slip of paper. "Tomorrow night. Ten o'clock." He goosed me, which I detest, but before I

could knee him, the door was flung open and Miss Cluff
looked in and blushed, for no discernible reason, and said,
"Welcome to the Music Department, Myra. We've all
been looking for you."

"Clem was playing me his score."

"He's so talented! Mr. Loner wants to see you right
away, it's urgent."

Buck was sitting with his feet on the desk and his Stetson over one eye. Since he made no move to sit up, much
less stand up, when I entered the room, I was obliged to
strike his feet a blow with my stout black leather handbag; they slid off the desk and onto the floor with a
crash.

"Stand up when a lady comes into the room, you son
of a bitch," I said but with a sweet tone not unlike Irene
Dunne in *The White Cliffs of Dover*.

"Lady!" He snorted. I leapt upon him, handbag raised
to strike again, but he managed with unexpected agility
to get to his feet and put the desk once more between us.
"You're nothing but some con-girl pretending to be married to my nephew when I got proof he never married
nobody. Here!" He thrust a legal document at me,
which I ignored. I knew that I had been careless, and
have been found out. My own fault.

"No record of my marriage to Myron exists in any of
the United States," I said, "for the excellent reason," I
wadded up the document and threw it at him, "that we
were married in Mexico."

"Whereabouts?"

"My lawyers will tell your lawyers," I said. "Meanwhile, if that settlement is not made by April first, I will

take over the whole shooting match." When in doubt, double the stakes, as James Cagney used to say.

I departed regally, but I was — am — shaken by the interview. I immediately rang my lawyer to assure him that I will be able to produce the marriage license as soon as a new one is issued at Monterrey.

Meanwhile — what a mess! Suddenly I feel terribly alone and afraid. My mood was hardly improved when I learned a few moments ago from a distraught Mary-Ann that Rusty has left town. When I pressed her as to why, she burst into tears and could not or would not say. I have never liked the month of February — even when the sun shines, as it does now, and it is warm.

20

My ground rules for the party were respected. I would wear bra and panties, unless otherwise inspired to remove them. Clem was forced to agree to this after I pointed out to him that in spite of his assurance to me no students would be present, Gloria Gordon was not only at the party but his hostess. My compromise was accepted. Give a little, get a little, as the saying goes.

The party was held in a small house high in the Hollywood Hills. I was driven there by a stocky monosyllabic man who was once a waiter at Romanoff's and could, if he chose, tell a thousand stories about the stars he waited on but instead spoke to me only of the weather and baseball. But then I think that he was probably stoned when he came to pick me up, and not at his conversational best.

When we arrived at the house, the door was opened by Clem, who wore nothing but glasses and a large door key on a chain about his neck. He is extremely hairy, which I don't like, and though he did not have an erection and so could not be fairly judged, his prick is small and rather dismal-looking as if too many people had chewed on it, and of course he is circumcised, which I find unattractive. Naturally, like so many physically underprivileged men, Clem regards himself as irresistible (no doubt some obscure psychological law of compensation is at work). He promptly took me in goatish arms, rammed his soft acorn against my pudendum, and bit my ear.

I stepped hard on his bare toes, and was promptly freed.

"Jesus, Myra!" He hopped on one foot, holding the other in his hand, a ludicrous sight that somewhat aroused me. I was even more aroused by Gloria who came to show me into the changing room. She, too, was nude with a body almost too beautiful for this world, slender and long, somewhat on the order of the early Jinx Falkenburg. As I undressed, it was all I could do not to take delicately in my hand one of those perfect rose-nippled breasts and simply hold it, worshipfully. Although I am not a Lesbian, I do share the normal human response to whatever is attractive physically in either sex. I say *normal* human response, realizing that our culture has resolutely resisted the idea of bisexuality. We insist that there is only one *right* way of having sex: man and woman joined together to make baby; all else is wrong. Worse, the neo-Freudian rabbis (of whom Dr. Montag is still one despite my efforts at conversion) believe that what they call heterosexuality is "healthy," that homosexuality is unhealthy, and that bisexuality is a myth despite their master Freud's stated conviction that all human beings are attracted to both sexes.

Intellectually, Dr. Montag is aware of the variety of normal human sexual response but, emotionally, no dentist from the Grand Concourse can ever accept the idea that a woman could or should find quite as much pleasure with her own sex as she does with men. Yet many women lead perfectly contented lives switching back and forth from male to female with a minimum of nervous wear and tear. But in the great tradition of neo-Freudian analysis, Dr. Montag refuses to accept any evidence that does not entirely square with his preconceptions. For him it is either Moses or the Golden Calf. There is no middle range. Yet he is often persuasive, even luminous, and for a time Myron fell under his spell just as Dr. Montag has since fallen under mine. Nevertheless, for all his limitations, it must never be forgotten that it was Randolph Spenser Montag who convinced Myron that one ought to live in consistent accordance with one's *essential* nature. As a result, on the Staten Island ferry, Myron acted out a dream of the absolute and like a Venetian Doge married that symbol of woman the sea but with his life, not a ring, leaving me to change the world alone.

Since that traumatic experience for us all, Randolph has been, in some ways, a new man, a changed dentist. Now he almost believes those stories his younger patients tell him of parties where sexual roles change rapidly, according to whim and in response to the moment's pleasure, stories he used to reject as wish-fulfillments. Between a beautiful girl and an unattractive man (between Gloria and Clem), I shall always be drawn, like any healthy-minded woman, to the girl, as I was last night when, very simply, I took both of Gloria's breasts in my hands and stooped to kiss the appendix scar just to the right of her navel, for all the world like a delicate dimple, so marvelously had the surgeon done his work.

"Chick, you are turning me on!" Gloria exclaimed as she flung my dress willy-nilly upon the bed with all the other clothes. Then she clutched at my panties, but I restrained her, reminding her of the agreement with Clem.

She frowned and pouted. "Not even for me?" she asked, fingering my lovely breasts already partially revealed through the lacy mesh of the bra.

"Later," I whispered, looking over Gloria's shoulder at my escort who was stripping down. It was evident that what he lacked in conversation he made up for in other ways. Beneath a not unpleasantly curved beer-belly, a large white object sprouted, as inviting to the touch as a well-wrought pitcher's handle.

On his way to the door, my hand snaked out and seized him, causing him to stop abruptly. I held him just long enough to achieve a small but exquisite sense of power (he was not able to move, so powerful is my grasp). Then I released him. Shouting "Crazy!" he vanished into the darkened room where the party was.

Impressions: varied, some pleasant, some not. All in all, *not* my sort of scene. I need one man to break down, not twenty to serve. But visually the scene was appealing. Mattresses spread at random across a tile floor. Towels hung from every lamp, giving a festive look to a room whose only light came from a single Moroccan lamp of intricately chased silver inset with red and blue glass.

Aesthetically, the decor was all that one could have wished and so were the girls; the men had seen to that. In fact, simply on circumstantial evidence, one could tell that a man had selected the guest list, for though there were several attractive young studs in the room (two of the five members of the Four Skins were present), the majority resembled Clem: physically unimpressive males forced to rely upon personality and money to get girls to bed. For my taste, they are exactly the wrong sort to have at an orgy, which, no doubt, is the reason why they are always the leading instigators of what is known locally as the "gangbang."

The party lasted four hours. That is as long as the male can hold out. Women of course can go on indefinitely if they are allowed occasional catnaps between orgasms. At one point Gloria experienced twelve orgasms in as many minutes (supplied her by the ex-waiter from Romanoff's, a really formidable man, capable of quite astonishing endurance and restraint); then she promptly fell asleep with her head in the lap of Clem, whom she had been attending to in an absentminded way. To his great alarm, she could not be awakened. Fortunately, we were able to pry her mouth open and salvage the tiny treasure before serious damage was done. Ten minutes later our Gloria was wide awake and ready for fun. This time Clem provided it. Having strapped on a formidable dildo because, as he said, "You got to have head," he was able to give

her maximum pleasure with a minimum of exertion on
his part.

My own participation was limited. I watched, and
only occasionally helped out: a tickle here, a pull there, a
lick, a bite, no more, except for one sudden rude intru-
sion from the rear which I did not see coming. It was one
of the Four Skins, a hillbilly type who explained to me, as
he was relieving himself, that he had first committed this
particular act at the age of twelve with a sheep and so, to
this day, he not only preferred back to front but sheep to
goats, or did he say girls? Like the rest of the Four Skins
his conversation is as difficult to understand as the lyrics
they sing. Had there been a pair of shears at hand, I
would have made a steer of him on the spot but since
there were not I did not, suffering in silence and even, to
be honest, deriving a certain perverse, masochistic, My-
ronesque enjoyment from the unlikely situation of Myra
Breckinridge, victorious Amazon, laid low.

Then, having discharged himself, the Skin abandoned
me and proceeded on his bully way. I shall of course take
my revenge upon him some day, somehow . . . even if I
must wait twenty years! Myra Breckinridge is impla-
cable and pitiless.

These graphic notes are really for your benefit, dear
Randolph. Examples of the way that the goyim you essentially despise behave (of course Clem is Jewish but he
has been entirely absorbed by California, that great
sponge into which all things are drawn and promptly
homogenized, including Judaism). Yet even you, with
your prejudices, could not help but be impressed at the

ease with which these young people let themselves go, without any apparent fear of commitment or of compromise. The males do not worry about acting out what the society believes to be the man's role (brutal, destructive, vagina-centered); they play with one another's bodies in a sportive way, and seem to have no secret dreams they dare not act out. All is in the open, or as one of them said to me as he rested on the floor between engagements, "After a scene like this I don't need it again for a week. I've had it, and there's nothing left I want, and I never feel so good like I do after a real party." So the Dionysian is still a necessity in our lives. Certainly its absence has made the world neurotic and mad. I am positive that access to this sort of pleasure in my adolescence would have changed me entirely. Fortunately, as it turned out, I was frustrated. If I had not been, Myra Breckinridge could never have existed, and the subsequent loss to the world of Myra, the self-creation, is something we, none of us, can afford at this time.

As I write these words, I suddenly think of Myron making love to Gloria Gordon! Why? How strange . . . just the thought of such a thing makes my eyes fill suddenly with tears. Poor Myron. Yet, all in all, he is better dead.

One must not underestimate the influence of these young people on our society. It is true that the swingers, as they are called, make up only a small minority of our society; yet they hold a great attraction for the young and bored who are the majority and who keep their sanity (those that do) by having a double sense of themselves. On the one hand, they must appear to accept without question our culture's myth that the male must be dominant, aggressive, woman-oriented. On the other hand, they are perfectly aware that few men are anything but slaves to an economic and social system that does not allow them to knock people down as proof of virility or in any way act out the traditional male role. As a result, the young men compensate by *playing* at being men, wearing cowboy clothes, boots, black leather, attempting through clothes (what an age for the fetishist!) to impersonate the kind of man our society *claims* to admire but swiftly puts down should he attempt to be anything more than an illusionist, playing a part.

It is the wisdom of the male swinger to know what he is: a man who is socially and economically weak, as much put upon by women as by society. Accepting his situation, he is able to assert himself through a polymorphic sexual abandon in which the lines between the sexes dissolve, to the delight of all. I suspect that this may be the only workable pattern for the future, and it is a most healthy one . . . certainly healthier than the rigid old-fashioned masculinity of someone like Rusty whose instinct to dominate in traditional ways is bound to end in defeat or frustration, excepting perhaps in his relations with the old-fashioned Mary-Ann . . . relations which are currently at an end, for she has still not heard from him, or so she says. I suspect he has been busted, and just as I was about to make my final move. It is too unfair!

The party ended in an orgy of eating. Delicate girls devoured cold cuts as though they had not been fed in weeks, while spent youths lay snoring among tangled towels that smelled of new-made love. How Myron would have enjoyed all this! Though I'm afraid he would have paid more attention to the boys than to the girls and perhaps imitated my bull-like Skin who, waiting until one young man had assumed the classic position between a girl's legs, leapt upon him and forced his way in, to the obvious irritation of the raped youth who, nevertheless, had sufficient aplomb (and Dionysian abandon) not to break his own stride, as it were — oh, how various are the ways of power!

BUCK LONER REPORTS —
Recording Disc No. 751 —
27 February

Well so far she has got the jump
on me this morning she came into my office and
gave me this Mexican wedding license apologizing
for not having got it sooner but it was mislaid Uncle
Buck I tell you when she calls me Uncle Buck like
that Id like to break her neck she is living hell and
theres no doubt about that she also said she was
getting impatient for her share of the estate and she
hoped quote mean old Flagler and Flagler would
soon see their way clear to the half million dollar
settlement unquote half million dollar settlement I
asked it was three fifty that we finally agreed on
before well she says quote that was before but I have
been kept waiting and waiting while your detectives
have been trying to get something on me like I was
criticizing General Motors or something and so I
regard the extra one fifty as damages for the mental
anguish you have been causing me unquote well I

controlled myself as best I could and said quote now
Myra you know what lawyers are and after all we
never did meet before and whats to keep a total
stranger from barging in and claiming to be mar
ried to my late nephew question mark end quote
oh I see your point of view she says in quotes of
course I do but you must also see mine and realize
just what it is I have been going through since My
ron died leaving me entirely alone in the world and
broke well we kicked that around the poor defense
less widow number and then she again gave me
until April one to pay up or else she goes to court
and really gets mean so I do my best to soothe her
putting the blame on Flagler and Flagler but the
thing is still fishy even though theres no doubt she
was involved deeply with Myron because though I
didnt know him I sure as hell knew Gertrude and at
one point Myra let slip the fact that she personally
had always found Gertrude hell particularly the way
she used to save worthless things like newspapers
and string and keep the icebox jammed with food
that had gone bad that she was too damned miserly
to throw out well Myra didnt make that up and we
both agreed that anybody who had a meal at Ger
trudes was courting ptomaine but then when I said
Gertrude really loved that boy of hers Myra frowned
and said oh no she didnt Uncle Buck she just loved
herself well dont we all I said no she said not to that
degree unquote but she wouldnt open up any more
obviously the two girls did not get on hard to say
which is the worst no not hard at all Myra is the
worst woman I have ever met exclamation mark
paragraph she then asked me if I had had news of
Rusty Godowsky and I said no but that our students
often disappear for a time like that and then show
up again like nothings happened but she said she

was concerned because of poor Mary Ann being so heartbroken Mary Ann hell Im sure Myras got her eye on that stud like half the girls on campus and is now demonstrating the edginess of a filly in heat anyway I said I would look into the matter of his disappearance beginning by calling up my friend the Sheriff a good Republican and ask him if the boy has been incarcerated in a hoosegow since he was on probation to begin with period paragraph then Myra asks me for permission to look at the medical reports on the students which are kept in my outer office and are private because quote I am doing some research on the I think she said post Rosen berg generation she is probably a Commie along with everything else but I have to handle little Miss Dynamite with kid gloves so I gave her permission after all theres nothing interesting in any of them reports just a routine physical checkup at the be ginning of their academic life we did consider once taking naked pictures like they do at Yale but the girls objected or to be exact the mothers and fathers of the girls objected even though this is the era of the Playboy bunny so that very good idea came to naught period paragraph change masseuses ap pointment from this afternoon to tomorrow as I must go in to town for a conference with Letitia Van Allen the best actors agent in this town for young stars of tomorrow having in her pocket practically her own key to casting at Universal dont forget to pick up sour cream for Bobbies beef Stroganoff

21

I am sitting beside Mary-Ann at the CBS television studio on Fairfax Avenue. Though it is only a caricature of a film studio, the ultimate effect is impressive. So impressive in fact that I am more than ever certain that the movies are now a mere subsidiary to this electronic device for projecting images around the world at, literally, the speed of light. What it will mean, I have not yet worked out. But it is now plain that the classic age of films has ended and will not return any more than verse drama, despite the wonder of the Jacobeans, has a chance of revival.

Of course visual narratives will always be filmed and shown if not in theatres on television. Yet the *nature* of those narratives is bound to change as television creates a new kind of person who will then create a new kind of art, a circle of creation that is only now just beginning. It is a thrilling moment to be alive! And though I yearn romantically for the classic films of the Forties, I know that they can never be reproduced since their era is as gone as the Depression, World War II and the national innocence which made it possible for Pandro S. Berman and a host of others to decorate the screens of tens of thousands of movie theatres with perfect dreams. There was a wholeness then which is lacking now and neither Alain Resnais nor Andy Warhol (the only film-makers of comparable stature today) can give us work which is not hopelessly fragmented. I except always Warhol's *Sleeping Man*, which broke new ground aesthetically and proved a radical theory I had always held but dared not openly formulate: that boredom in the arts can be, under the right circumstances, dull.

I find it altogether too satisfying to be sitting beside Mary-Ann in the audience that has been assembled for the Art Linkletter Show. An M.C. is trying to warm us up with bad jokes. In a few minutes we shall be on the air, performers, technicians, audience, viewers — all made one by the magic of the tube. I find this particular show absolutely unbearable, preferring as I do the *total* electronic effect of, let us say, Milton Berle. But I am here because Mary-Ann wanted me to come and I usually do what she wants me to do for we are now curiously united by Rusty's disappearance. Of course she continues to believe that I dislike him and think him an ape, and I do nothing to disabuse her of this notion. I find almost unbearable the painful sweetness of knowing that I shall one day possess, in my own way, what she believes to be entirely hers, assuming of course that Rusty ever returns.

Mary-Ann believes that if he is not in prison (the likeliest possibility since a boy with a police record is prone to constant false arrest in the Los Angeles area where only professional criminals are safe from harassment by the local police), he has gone off with some of his wild friends, possibly to Mexico. I do my best to soothe her, and we have long "girl-talks" about men and life . . . and about her career.

Unlike the other students, Mary-Ann could be professional. Miss Cluff is absolutely right and I for one would like to cut a corner or two and present her directly to an agent, instead of waiting until June, the usual time for the students to show what they can do which, traditionally, is not much. Miss Cluff tells me that in the seven years that she has been at the Academy no student has ever got a job on television or appeared in a film. This is a remarkable record. Some do get jobs modeling but that is often just plain whoring.

When I asked Buck about the dismal showing his students make in the professional world, he seemed not at all taken aback. "Honey," he said, knowing how much I hate to be called "honey," resembling, in this, the former First Lady, "what matters is making people happy and while the kids are here they are happy. Now there is, I am willing to admit, a real letdown come June when our kids realize that the outside world of show biz is a big cruel place with maybe no place for them. Yes, I admit that's an awful thing for them to find out and I've even toyed with the idea of never allowing any agents or professional people to come to the June exercises but of course if I really kept them away I'd go out of business, so we all have to suffer through the June Letdown which

is immediately followed by the Buck Loner July Spectacular which is a series of awards based closely on the
actual Academy Awards, with many Oscars (or Bucks as
the kids call them) to be given out by some real-life celebrity on the order of Bobby Darin and that, let me tell
you, sure as hell makes up for June."

"Yes, but sooner or later they will *have* to go out into
the world . . ."

"Why?" The question was straightforward. "As long
as they scrounge up enough money to pay the tuition
they can stay here for life. Look at Irving Amadeus. He
came here fourteen years ago as a student to become a
singing star on the order of Paul Robeson and he is with
us still, on the staff now as an invaluable teacher with
over *three hundred recordings* to his credit. If that isn't
as good as being a real star I don't know what is!"

This curiously hateful philosophy has made Buck
Loner rich. But then, to be honest, all that I care about at
the moment is my share of his wealth. That and Mary-
Ann's career which she does not take seriously. "Only
one star in the family," she keeps quoting Rusty. To
which I invariably reply, "You're the star. He's the garage mechanic."

I have now got Mary-Ann to the point where she will
at least audition for an agent before June, and that means
I must start making the rounds myself, trying to find the
best person to handle her. Although her voice has a classic tone like Jeanette MacDonald (and so of no use in the
current market), she also has a second more jazzy voice
not unlike that of the late La Verne, the most talented of

the Andrews Sisters. I am certain that if she were to develop her La Verne-voice she could, with her remarkable appearance acting as opening wedge, become a star.

Last night I played several Andrews Sisters records for her and though she had never before heard of the Andrews Sisters (!), she conceded that their *tone* was unusual — which is understating the matter! Their tone is unique and genuinely mythic, a part of the folklore of the best years of the American past. They really did roll out that barrel, and no one has yet rolled it back.

Mary-Ann has just nudged my arm. "Really, Miss Myra, you musn't write like that in public!" She chides me gently, for to write in public in the electronic age is to commit an antisocial obscenity.

To please her, I shall now put away this notebook and listen to the jokes of the comedian as he responds to the sterile laughter of the studio audience of which I am a part, for we are suddenly all of us — such a pleasure — on the air!

22

Just as I expected, seventy-two per cent of the male students are circumcised. At Clem's party I had been reminded of the promiscuous way in which American doctors circumcise males in childhood, a practice I highly disapprove of, agreeing with that publisher who is forever advertising in the New York *Times Book Review* a work which proves that circumcision is necessary for only a very few men. For the rest, it constitutes, in the advertiser's phrase, "a rape of the penis." Until the Forties, only the upper or educated classes were circumcised in America. The *real* people were spared this humiliation. But during the affluent postwar years the operation became standard procedure, making money for doctors as well as allowing the American mother to mutilate her son in order that he might never forget her early power over him. Today only the poor Boston Irish, the Midwestern Poles and the Appalachian Southerners can be counted upon to be complete.

Myron never forgave Gertrude for her circumcision of him. In fact, he once denounced her in my presence for it. She defended herself by saying that the doctor had recommended it on hygienic grounds — which of course does not hold water since most foreskins are easily manipulated and kept clean. What is truly sinister is the fact that with the foreskin's removal, up to fifty per cent of sensation in the glans penis is reduced . . . a condition no doubt as pleasing to the puritan American mother as it is to her co-conspirator, the puritan Jewish doctor who delights in being able to mutilate the goyim in the same vivid way that his religion (and mother!) mutilated him.

I once had the subject out with Dr. Montag, who granted me every single point and yet, finally, turned dentist and confessed, "Whenever I hear the word 'smegma,' I become physically ill." I am sure Moses is roasting in hell, along with Jesus, Saint Paul, and Gertrude Percey Breckinridge.

I was not able to find Rusty's medical report and so do not know whether or not he has been circumcised. I hope not for I prefer the penis intact . . . in order that it be raped not by impersonal surgery but by me!

23

In an alcove at the back of the cafeteria Buck Loner often has lunch with some notable he would like the students to observe at close hand. Today it was the famous agent Letitia Van Allen, and so I joined them, to Buck's ill-disguised fury. Miss Van Allen is a handsome vigorous woman of perhaps forty, with steely gray eyes. We got on famously, to Buck's chagrin.

"Talent is not what Uncle Buck and I deal in, Miss Van Allen," I said, lightly resting my hand on Buck's clenched fist. "We deal in *myths*. At any given moment the world requires one full-bodied blonde Aphrodite (Jean Harlow), one dark siren of flawless beauty (Hedy Lamarr), one powerful inarticulate brute of a man (John Wayne), one smooth debonair charmer (Melvyn Douglas), one world-weary corrupt lover past his prime (Humphrey Bogart), one eternal good-sex woman-wife Myrna Loy), one wide-eyed chicken boy (Lon McCallister), one gentle girl singer (Susanna Foster), one win-

ning stud (Clark Gable), one losing stud outside the law
(James Cagney), and so on. Olympus supports many
gods and goddesses and they are truly eternal, since
whenever one fades or falls another promptly takes his
place, for the race requires that the pantheon be always
filled. So what we are looking for — and what you, Miss
Van Allen, have *found* time and again — are those
mythic figures who, at the right moment, can be placed
upon their proper pedestal. For instance, since the death
of Marilyn Monroe, no blonde voluptuous goddess has
yet appeared to take her place and so, if I were creating
stars, I would look for a girl who most filled that particular bill, who could be the lost Golden Girl. In fact, as in
any other business, we must begin with market research.
This means carefully analyzing Olympus to find out
which archetypal roles are temporarily vacant and who
are the contenders. At the moment the suave male seducer is in great supply while the befuddled normal man
next door, filled with ludicrous fantasies, is a drug on the
market, what with at least one and a half Jack Lemmon
pictures each year. But the blonde goddess, the dark goddess, the singing girl and the inarticulate hero are each
currently in need of someone to make of the divine spirit
living flesh as well as eternal celluloid. At this very moment, perhaps in this very room, there are unknown boys
and girls destined to be — for the length of a career —
like gods, if only we can find and reveal them. That is
why you and I, Letitia — I may call you that? — are similar to those Tibetan priests who upon the death of the
Dalai Lama must seek out his reincarnation. And so, like
priestesses, despite all personal hardship, we must con-

stantly test and analyze the young men and women of
America in order to find the glittering few who are immortal, who are the old, the permanent gods of our race
reborn."

There was a long silence when I finished. Buck toyed
with his icebox cake while Letitia Van Allen simply
stared at me. Then she said, "That is the damnedest, truest thing I've ever heard said about this lousy racket.
Come on, let's have a drink. Buck, give us a drink in that
office of yours, you old bastard!" She took me by the
arm. "He's far and away the biggest con-man in the business, but from where I sit it looks like he may have met
his match. You've got quite a line and, as a fellow con-
girl, I would like to give it some study." I had made, as I
intended, an enormous impression.

Over a beaker of Scotch in Buck's office, Letitia told
me in no uncertain terms that if I ever wanted to leave
Buck there was a place in her office for a go-getter like
me.

Buck brightened when he heard this. "Why, honey,
that sounds just swell, don't it? This is too little a pond
for a talent like yours." To which I replied demurely, "It
may be a small pond but it's ours, Uncle Buck, yours and
mine (you see, Letitia, I'm a half-owner of the property), and I could never let Uncle Buck down." Buck's
face shut with a snap.

Miss Van Allen missed this exchange, for I had just
given her some photographs of Mary-Ann Pringle.
"Pretty girl. But no Marilyn Monroe." She gave the pictures back.

"It's her voice," I explained. "That's what makes her a

possible immortal. She is the Singing Girl Goddess, waiting for the chance to reveal herself."

"They're not making that kind of picture right now. But maybe she could work up a nightclub act or get in the road show of some Broadway musical. Anyway, on your say-so, I'll listen to her — but not now. What about studs?" Letitia, I fear, is a monosexual. Only men arouse her.

"We got some swell kids . . ." began Buck but I cut him short. "There's one — *maybe*. Category: Inarticulate Hero. His name is Rusty Godowsky . . ."

"That name has got to go and so do I." Letitia turned to me. "Come see me the first of the week, Myra . . . lunch . . . I'll pick your brains. You Easterners have all the kinky angles that are *in* right now. That's what I keep telling them at Universal: 'Don't be so California, for God's sake! California's square, while the world is full of kinks as yet undreamed of in the Greater Los Angeles Area.' Then she was gone.

I could not help but rub it in. "Stick with me," I said to the crestfallen Buck, "and maybe some of your students will work in show biz."

Before he could answer, the masseuse arrived: a spectacular Eurasian in a white nurse's uniform. As we parted, I reminded him of our deadline. Either he has paid me my share in full by April 1 or we up the ante.

BUCK LONER REPORTS —
Recording Disc No. 763 —
4 March
        Things are coming to a head at least if
they dont I dont know if I can stand it much longer
with the new masseuse it took over an hour which
is a sign of something and that something is Myra
Breckinridge archfiend Flagler and Flagler are doing
their best they say to get something on Myra but so
far nothing at all they are even bugging her telephone
and just now sent over this tape which may be signifi
cant or so they think of her talking long distance to
a New York headshrinker called Randolph Montag
his tape is herewith enclosed or included or what
ever you call it

The Golden State Detective Agency submits the
following unedited telephone conversation with the
understanding that the contents of same are highly
confidential and Golden State assumes no responsi
bility whatsoever for having obtained said property.

OPERATOR: Los Angeles calling Dr. Rudolph Moon
. . . what's the name again, dear?

MYRA: Montag, Randolph not Rudolph Montag,
and why don't you . . .

OPERATOR: Los Angeles calling Dr. Moondog . . .
is he there?

VOICE: Mummy [two words not audible] later
[three to four words not audible] the cat's sick . . .

OPERATOR: Little boy, could you tell your daddy
this is Los Angeles . . .

MYRA: Damn it, Dr. Montag is not married . . .

OPERATOR: . . . Los Angeles calling and . . .

VOICE: . . . threw up all over the floor . . .

MYRA: God damn it, operator, you've got the wrong
number . . .

OPERATOR: I hear you, miss, you don't have to
shout . . .

MYRA: The number is . . .

OPERATOR: . . . I will redial the number, miss.

ELECTRONIC SOUNDS: heavy breathing of operator and / or Myra.

VOICE: This is a recording. The number you have
just dialed is not a working number . . .

MYRA: Operator, please I don't have all day . . .

OPERATOR: Apparently the number you gave me
is not a working number . . .

MYRA: Dial it again, damn it! You silly [word not
clearly audible].

VOICE: Yes?

OPERATOR: Los Angeles calling Dr. Rupert Moonman, are you him?

VOICE: Yes, yes. This is Dr. Moonman, I mean
Montag, who is calling he . . . ?

MYRA: Randolph, this is Myra . . .

OPERATOR: Your party is on the line, Miss . . .

MYRA: I haven't written because I've been . . .

OPERATOR: *Dr. Moon is on the line* . . .

MYRA: I know he is, now will you kindly get off . . .

MONTAG: Who is calling him again?

MYRA: It's Myra Breckinridge, you idiot!

MONTAG: Myra! This is a real pleasure . . .

MYRA: . . . didn't write because so much work to do . . .

MONTAG: . . . so how's the weather out there?

MYRA: . . . need your help . . .

MONTAG: . . . cold here, maybe twelve above zero which is why the ten o'clock patient missed her hour so I can talk . . .

MYRA: . . . about this damned inheritance . . .

MONTAG: . . . how is your dental health?

MYRA: Never been better, as a matter of fact we are on the verge of a real mental breakthrough which should . . .

MONTAG: I meant how are your teeth? That impacted wisdom tooth that was giving us so much trouble . . .

MYRA: For God's sake, Randolph, don't waste the three minutes talking about teeth . . . they're O.K. . . .

MONTAG: Good dental health means good mental health . . .

MYRA: . . . what I want is this: for you to say you were a witness to my marriage, in Monterrey, Mexico. And, God knows, in the truest sense you were and are . . .

MONTAG: At a certain level of course I am a witness and will gladly say so but there's also the legal aspect . . .

MYRA: . . . have to do is come out here and at a

crucial moment which may or may not arise say you were present when I married Myron, which you were. . . .

MONTAG: . . . I suppose this all has to do with Gertrude's property . . .

MYRA: . . . swine Buck Loner is trying to do me out of a settlement, and so he wants to prove we were never really married . . .

MONTAG: . . . thinking about poor Myron the other day . . .

MYRA: You might think about *me* for a change. . . .

MONTAG: . . . projecting hostility again, must be careful . . .

MYRA: . . . am in trouble, Myron's dead . . .

MONTAG: Myron was a Christ figure . . .

MYRA: Luckily he found the right doctor with the two sticks of wood and the three nails . . .

MONTAG: . . . need help again. Can't you come back here for a few sessions . . .

MYRA: I'm broke and this conversation is breaking me so will you do what I ask . . .

MONTAG: Naturally only . . .

MYRA: In writing!

MONTAG: Is that necessary?

MYRA: It may have to be. Well? Cat got your tongue?

MONTAG: No, I was lighting a cigar, oral gratification is called for at moments of discomfort . . .

MYRA: Are you uncomfortable?

MONTAG: Naturally, Myra. Who wouldn't be in the spot you've put me in? After all our relationship is a good deal more than that of just analyst and patient. I am also your dentist and have your best interests at heart. Yes, of course I will *say* I was a witness to the marriage with the proviso . . .

MYRA: No proviso unless you want to have your
license as a lay analyst revoked in the State of New
York for gross malpractice . . .
MONTAG: I detect *a great deal* of hostility, Myra, in
your voice . . .
MYRA: . . . then it's a deal. This is costing mon-
ey . . .
MONTAG: Of course I'll help but . . .
MYRA: Goodbye, Randolph. . . .
End of tape.

BUCK LONER REPORTS —
Recording Disc No. 763 —
(continued)
                          Something obviously fishy but
what question mark Myra probably was married in
Monterrey from the sound of what they were saying
to each other but why is that doctor so nervous and
unwilling to put his John Hancock to any sort of
document I will tell Flagler and Flagler to put the
heat on this doctor because I must find out the truth
or die in the attempt not to mention losing half this
place which I built up from nothing period para
graph well I couldve been knocked over with a
feather when Letitia Van Allen who I used to boff
in the old days and was also a good friend to Bobbie
Dean took a shine to Myra who barged in on our
lunch in the cafeteria and promptly began one of
her endless speeches which drive me up the wall
like they say but Letitia who is easily the toughest
dame in this town with the key to casting at Univer
sal in her pocket and not one youd think to be taken
in by nutty highbrow Eastern talk well Myra did her
work and the two girls are now bosom buddies
which is not good for yours truly which is why
everything depends now on nailing Myra Breckin

ridge once and for all question what about framing her with drugs maybe no she would still get the money even in jail God damn it buy chicory for Bobbie

24

Letitia Van Allen has heard the voice of Mary-Ann! And loved it! Yesterday I met Letitia at her offices on Melrose Avenue which occupy an entire Greek revival house, reminiscent of Tara, the late David O. Selznick's trademark. All the rooms are furnished in such a way as to suggest a gracious Southern mansion, not a talent agency. Letitia's private office (we are now on a first-name basis) is a lovely large airy second-floor bedroom-cum-boudoir, a most unusual setting for a famous agent yet somehow entirely suitable for her. Letitia works at a Dutch provincial writing desk in an alcove within view of the four-poster bed at the far end of the room. The effect is enchanting.

The salad and cottage cheese lunch was less charming (I have developed an extraordinary appetite lately and must for the first time in my life worry about becoming heavy). We talked of everything, and found many areas of agreement. She believes I would make a formidable agent and I have no doubt that she is right but I prefer to go my own solitary way as critic and mythmaker, and of course as explicator of the mind of Parker Tyler. Like Myron, I am in the tradition of Mortimer Brewster, the drama critic in *Arsenic and Old Lace*, a man for whom, as Tyler puts it so superbly, "the facts of *lunacy*, *virginity*, and *death*, the last a mask for *impotence*, are inseparable."

Over a dry martini *after* lunch (Letitia, I suspect, has a drinking problem), we listened to a record of Mary-Ann singing a number of songs of the Forties, selected by me and arranged by Miss Cluff. Letitia listened with eyes narrowed. When the record was finished, she again asked for photographs. I gave them to her. She studied them for a long time. "O.K.," she said, "I'll meet her. Make an appointment with my secretary, any free time next week." Then Letitia put her feet up on a Regency bench. "Why're you pushing this kid?"

"She has talent. So few people do."

"But according to your theory, that will probably count against her. Now if you don't mind my asking a personal question, you aren't perhaps involved with her on a more *personal* level?"

I blushed for the first time in some years. "If you mean am I a dike, no. Not at all. Quite the contrary. Actually I'm interested in her because of her boyfriend who happens to have skipped town and I feel sorry for her. . . ."

"There's nothing wrong with being a dike, you know." Letitia blew smoke rings thoughtfully. For an instant I wondered if perhaps I had not got her range. But she quickly assured me that my first impression of her

had been the right one. "That bed," she said, indicating
the four-poster with a swagger stick, "has held just about
every stud in town who wants to be an actor. Do I shock
you, Myra?"

"How can you shock me when you are just like me?
The new American woman who uses men the way they
once used women."

"Jesus, Myra, but you are *quick!* What a team we'd
make. Sure you don't want another martini? It's just
water now in the shaker. Well, then I'll have it." She
poured herself a full glass. "Listen, dear, if you find anything really interesting at that circus of no-talent Buck's
conducting, send him over for a chat with Letitia."

"With pleasure."

"And you come along, too." Letitia flashed a brilliant
smile which I answered with one equally brilliant. Two
masterful women had met and there is no man alive capable of surviving our united onslaught. Like had been attracted to like from the first moment we met and though
it was now plain that she expected me to supply her with
studs, I was not in the least distressed at being so used.
Women like ourselves owe it to one another to present a
united front to the enemy. Meanwhile, as quid for my
pro, she will try to find work for Mary-Ann. All in all, as
satisfying an encounter as I have had since Dr. Montag
first introduced himself to us at the Blue Owl Grill.

25

Is it possible to describe anything accurately? That is the problem set us by the French New Novelists. The answer is, like so many answers to important questions, neither yes nor no. The treachery of words is notorious. I write that I "care for" Mary-Ann. But what does that *mean?* Nothing at all because I do not care for her at all times or at any time in all ways. To be precise (the task set us in the age of science), as I sit here at the card table in my room, wearing an old dressing gown of Myron's, I can say that I like her eyes and voice but not her mouth (too small) or hands (too blunt). I could fill many pages of yes-no and still not bring the reader to any *deep* knowledge of what it is I feel at 7:10 P.M., March 12. It is impossible to sort out all one's feelings at any given moment on any given subject, and so perhaps it is wise never to take on any subject other than one's own protean but still manageable self.

What does Mary-Ann think of me? I could not begin to do more than guess nor, I suppose, could she answer this question even to herself: liking, hostility, attraction, revulsion, self-aggrandizement, self-sacrifice, all mingled together with no clear motif save the desire of each to exert power over the other. That is the one human constant, to which all else is tributary.

Dr. Montag still challenges my theory from time to time. Once he spoke of the maternal instinct as something *not* involving power. But of course it does, in the most obvious way: the teat (or bottle) is the source of life to the baby, to be given or withheld at the mother's pleasure. If there is any more fulfilling way of achieving total power over another human being, I have yet to hear of it. Of course most people successfully disguise their power drives, particularly from themselves. Yet the will to prevail is constant and unrelenting. Take that charming, seemingly unaggressive man who makes apparently idle jokes that cause others to laugh. In a sly way, he is exerting power quite as much as Hitler did: after all, his listeners were not laughing until he *made* them laugh. Thus it goes, at every level. My own uniqueness is simply the result of self-knowledge. *I know what I want and I know what I am*, a creation of my own will, now preparing for a breakthrough into an area where, until Myron's death, I could enter only in dreams. Having already destroyed subjectively the masculine principle, I must now shatter it objectively in the person of Rusty, who has reappeared.

But who am I? What do I feel? Do I exist at all? That

is the unanswerable question. At the moment I feel like the amnesiac in *Spellbound*, aware that something strange is about to happen. I am apprehensive; obscurely excited

26

The telephone just rang. It was Mary-Ann. I have
never heard her so excited. "He's back! Rusty's back!" I
allowed her to think that she was telling me something
that I did not know. In actual fact, late this afternoon,
Irving Amadeus told me, "That beautiful creature just
showed up for Atavistic Rhythm, and here we'd all given
him up for lost!"

I went straight to Buck's office and checked with the
secretary, who was at first reluctant to give me details,
but when I threatened to take the matter up with Buck
himself, she told me that Rusty had been arrested with
two other young men at the Mexican border and held on
suspicion of smuggling marijuana into the States. Fortunately, there was no very compelling evidence against
them, and they were let go. Nevertheless, Rusty's period
of probation has been extended, and the probation officer
has asked Buck to keep an eye on him.

But Rusty had told Mary-Ann none of this. "You see,

he was with these wild boys in Mexico and their car broke down and they were too broke to pay even for a bus ticket and so the American consul finally bailed them out, after they were practically starving to death." No doubt about it, Rusty is very much a man of his era: his fantasy life shields Mary-Ann as well as himself from the cruel disorders of reality.

Though I cannot say that the pleasure of others has ever had any effect upon me except to produce a profound melancholy, I was *almost* pleased at Mary-Ann's delight. "You must be very happy," I whispered like Phyllis Thaxter in *Thirty Seconds over Tokyo*, with wonderful Van Johnson.

"And we want to have dinner with you tonight, if that's all right. I told him how simply wonderful you've been to me while he was gone."

"I'm sure you'd rather have him all to yourself tonight. Besides, are you sure he wants to see me?"

There was a light hesitation, followed by much protestation to the effect that Rusty was really very admiring of me since I had been such a help to him in Posture class.

27

It is now midnight. In many ways, a most exciting evening. I met Mary-Ann and Rusty at the Cock and Bull on the Strip; as one might guess, it is Rusty's favorite restaurant for the food is profoundly hearty. He was unusually exuberant and for once I did not seem to make him uneasy. He improvised freely about his adventures in Mexico, all the while eating scones smeared with raspberry jam. I toyed with a single slice of turkey. I am in danger of becoming fat like Gertrude, who resembled, in her last days, a spoiled pear.

"Then after we left Tijuana, we had to break up because, you see, three guys can't hitchhike together. Nobody would pick up three guys looking like us, with beards and all dirty, though there was this one fruit . . ." Rusty frowned at the pseudo-memory or, more likely, at an actual recollection transposed to flesh out the current fantasy. "He was willing to give us a lift, this funny little Mexican with shiny gold teeth and so nervous those gold teeth was chattering but he wanted us real bad, but we said hell no, I mean who wants to go that route?"

"Many do," I said casually, in such a way that I did not seem to be challenging him. Under the table I gave Mary-Ann's hand a little squeeze which she gratefully returned.

Rusty nodded wisely, mouth full. "Yeah, I know. Why there are some guys — some guys I know right at school — who'll sell their ass to some fruit for twenty bucks, just because they're too lazy to get a job."

"But wouldn't *you* do that, if you needed the money?"

"Hell, I'd starve first, and that's the truth." He pulled Mary-Ann close to him and gave her a kiss. I believed him.

In a sense, Rusty is a throwback to the stars of the Forties, who themselves were simply shadows cast in the bright morning of the nation. Yet in the age of the television commercial he is sadly superfluous, an anachronism, acting out a masculine charade that has lost all meaning. That is why, to save him (and the world from his sort), I must change entirely his sense of himself.

When Rusty had finally completed his story of having been down-and-out in Mexico (borrowing heavily from a recent television drama on the same theme), we spoke of Mary-Ann and the good impression that she had made on Letitia Van Allen. Even the unworldly Rusty was impressed. "Do you *really* think she likes Mary-Ann?"

"Very much."

"Oh, not that much." Although a Kathryn Grayson singing star, Mary-Ann also belongs to the Joan Leslie tradition of self-effacing good-sex woman-wife. For her it is Rusty's career that matters, not her own. "Anyway," she said, "it's all due to Miss Myra. She arranged the whole thing."

"That was a swell thing to do." Rusty's voice was deep and warm and he gave me a level gaze reminiscent of James Craig in the fourth reel of *Marriage Is a Private Affair*. "A mighty swell thing, and we're both as grateful as we can be," he added, carefully putting the two of them together on one side, leaving me alone on the other.

"Who Miss Van Allen should really see is Rusty," said Mary-Ann, predictably, to which I replied, as predictably, "Of course she'll see him, but in June. Don't worry, I've already told her about him."

"That's real nice of you. . . ." He was overcome by sincerity like James Stewart in any movie. Then the large veined hands with the blunt fingers took yet another scone and covered it with jam, and I meditated on the dark journey of those veins inside the jacket as they proceeded up the marbled forearms, coiling about the thick biceps, vanishing finally in the deep armpits.

What would Myron have thought of him? Probably not much. Myron preferred the sinister and vicious, the totally abandoned. Rusty is not only not abandoned, he would not have been available, even to Myron whose technique as a seducer was highly developed. Yet where Myron would have failed I shall succeed.

The fact that Rusty has not an inkling of my plans makes every moment we spend together in Mary-Ann's company exquisite. Also, the deliberate (on my part) manipulation of the conversation was curiously thrilling, affording me an opportunity to observe how something entirely alien behaves in its native habitat: the never-fulfilled desire of the dedicated anthropologist who real-izes that the moment he arrives in a village to study its culture, that culture has already been subtly altered by the simple fact of his presence; just as the earthly mi-crobes our astronauts are certain to let loose upon other worlds are sure to kill or change those extraterrestrial forms of life we would most like to preserve in order to understand. But then it is our peculiar fate to destroy or change all things we touch since (and let us never forget it) *we* are the constant and compulsive killers of life, the mad dogs of creation, and our triumphant viral progress can only end in a burst of cleansing solar fire, either simu-lated by us or thrust upon us by the self-protective mechanism of a creation that cannot for long endure too many violent antibodies within its harmonious system. Death and destruction, hate and rage, these are the most characteristic of human attributes, as Myra Breckinridge knows and personifies but soon means, in the most ex-traordinary way, entirely to transcend.

Yet the presence of the anthropologist (me) at the wooden table in the Cock and Bull did, eventually, alter significantly the behavior of the two natives as they lost their self-consciousness to the degree that the conversa-tion ceased to be particular and became general, some-thing that almost never happens among the lower orders who are, to a man, walking autobiographers, reciting their dull memoirs at extraordinary length, oblivious to the extent they bore even others of their kind who, of course, wait impatiently to tell *their* stories.

Somehow the subject reverted to Rusty's proud rejection of the Mexican's advances, and Mary-Ann made it plain that for her part she could never consider making love to another woman. "It just . . . well, disgusts me," she said. "I mean I just *couldn't*. I think, well, a woman should act like a woman and a man should act like a man, and that's that."

"But *how* should a man act?" I was mild.

Rusty knew. "He should ball chicks, that's how he should act."

"But only if he really loves them." Mary-Ann was droll; both laughed at what was obviously a private joke.

"And *why* should he ball chicks?" I continued my gentle catechism.

"Well, because that's . . . well, Christ, it's *natural!*"

"And that's how you get babies," said Mary-Ann sagely. "I mean that's how nature intended it."

"Do you think nature intended you to have a baby each time you make love?"

Mary-Ann looked like a lapsed Catholic, trying to recall what she had been taught. But Rusty was a good Catholic Pole and knew right from wrong. "That's what you're *supposed* to do, yes. That's what we're told in church."

"But you do use contraceptives, don't you?"

Both flushed, and Rusty said, "Well, sure. I guess most Catholics do now, but that doesn't mean you don't know it's wrong."

"Then you basically believe that it's right for more

and more babies to be born, even though half the people ever born in the world are now alive, and that each day twelve thousand people starve to death in India and South America?" Oh, the sly Myra Breckinridge! Nothing can escape the fine net of her dialectic!

Rusty frowned to show that he was thinking when actually, as one of the acting-students recently said of another's performance, he was only thinking he was thinking. "Well, maybe those Indians and Chinese and so on should probably practice birth control since their religion doesn't care, if they have one . . ."

"But they do have religions. And they do care. And they believe that for a man to be manly he must have as many children as possible . . ."

"Because so many babies die in childbirth." Mary-Ann was unusually thoughtful.

"They used to die," I said. "And that kept the population in a proper balance with the food supply. But now the children live. And starve. And all because their parents passionately believe that to be manly is to make babies and to be womanly is to bear them."

"But we're different." Rusty was dogged. "We got enough food and we also have . . ."

"Family planning." Mary-Ann looked happy. No doubt contemplating some planning of her own.

"Enough food," however, was all the cue I needed. I was brilliant. I quoted the best of the world's food authorities (famine for us all by 1974 and forget about plankton and seaweed: not enough of it). I demonstrated that essentially Malthus had been right, despite errors of calculation. I described what happens to rats when they

are crowded in too small a place: their kidneys deterio-
rate, and they go mad. I told how whenever the food
supply of the lemmings is endangered, a majority of the
race drown themselves in order that those left behind
may flourish.

Then I gave statistics for the current world death rate,
showing how it has drastically declined in the last fifty
years due to advanced medicine. The physically and
mentally weak who ordinarily would have died at birth
now grow up to become revolutionaries in Africa, Asia
and Harlem. As a result of miracle drugs and incontinent
breeding, the world's food supply can no longer support
the billions of people alive at present; there will of course
be even less food for those thousands who are joining us
every minute. What is to be done? How is the race to be
saved (I did not go into the more profound question of
whether or not it *should* be saved)? My answer was simple enough: famine and war are now man's only hope.
To survive, human population must be drastically reduced. Happily, our leaders are working instinctively toward that end, and there is no doubt in my mind that
nature intends Lyndon Johnson and Mao Tse-tung to be
the agents of our salvation. By destroying a majority of
the human race, they will preserve the breed since the
survivors are bound to be not only wiser than we but
racially stronger as a result of cellular mutancies caused
by atomic radiation. If I say so myself, I had my listeners'
eyes bugging out by the time I had sketched for them
man's marvelous if fiery fate.

"But what can we do to *stop* all this from happening?"
Mary-Ann was plainly alarmed.

"Don't have children. That is the best thing. A gesture of course, but better than nothing. And try to change your attitudes about what is normal." Then, in quick succession, I delivered a number of anthropological hay-makers. Proper womanly behavior for an Eskimo wife is to go to bed with anyone her husband brings back to the igloo. Proper manly behavior for the Spartan warrior was to make love to a boy while teaching him how to be a soldier. I gave a rapid review of what is considered proper sexual behavior in Polynesia and along the Amazon. Everything I said came as revelation to Rusty and Mary-Ann, and they were obviously horrified by the *un*-naturalness of what was considered natural in other parts of the world. I believe I planted a seed or two. Mary-Ann of course could never prostitute herself like an Eskimo wife nor could Rusty ever make love to an adolescent boy ("those teeny-boppers give me a pain"); yet each now regards his old certainties as being, at least, relative. That is progress.

As could be expected, it was Mary-Ann who mounted the counterattack. "Maybe you're right when you say there's nothing that's really *basically* normal but when everybody tells you that they want you to behave in a certain way, like marrying one man and having only his children, isn't that the *right* thing to do because doesn't the society deep down *know* what it's doing, and is trying to protect itself?"

Unexpectedly she had made a good point. Not once in all these weeks have I suspected her of possessing a true intelligence. Obviously I have been misled by her California manner which is resolutely cretinous as well as nasal. The possibility that she might one day be a woman I could actually talk to was a revelation, and by no means an unpleasant one. Naturally, she could not be allowed to *win* her point. Even so, it will, as we academics say, count against the final grade.

I challenged her with a simple question: does any society know how to preserve itself? I then listed a number of civilizations that had destroyed themselves through upholding customs that were self-destructive. For instance, the health of the Roman state depended upon a vigorous aristocracy but that aristocracy committed suicide by insisting that their cooking be done in expensive pots made of lead. The result was acute lead poisoning which led to impotence and the literal extinction of an entire class, killed by custom. Then, superb dialectician that I am, I discussed every society's *secret* drive to destroy itself and whether or not this was a good thing, taken in the larger context of the human race's evolution. They were both shocked at the idea, particularly when I brought it home to them by suggesting that Rusty's desire to have sex only with girls and Mary-Ann's desire to have at least four children the world did not need might be considered proof that our society is now preparing to kill itself by exhausting the food supply and making nuclear war inevitable. Should this be the case, the only alternative (and a most unlikely one) would be for all the Rustys to follow the Spartan custom of making love to boys while the Mary-Anns, as lovers of women, would at least help preserve the race by bringing no more children into the world. But of course I was playing devil's advocate since I am secretly convinced that we shall soon be purged by a chiliastic fire, and so, in the long run, current behavior will best serve us by hastening our necessary end. Yet efforts must still be made to preserve life, to change the sexes, to re-create Man. There is an off chance that my mission may yet succeed.

Mary-Ann was most depressed.

I took her hand in mine. "Don't worry," I said. "What will happen will happen. Meanwhile, all I ask is that you be happy . . . and you, too, Rusty." I gave him a beautiful yet knowing smile like Ann Sothern in the first of the Maisie films. "But to be *truly* happy, I think you must both begin to think a little bit about changing your sexual attitudes, becoming more open, less limited, abandoning old-fashioned stereotypes of what is manly and what is feminine. As it is, if you, Rusty, should ever find a boy sexually interesting, you might or might not do something about it but whatever you did do or did not do you'd certainly feel guilty because you've been taught that to be a man is to be physically strong, self-reliant, and a lover of girls, one at a time."

"So what's wrong with that?" Rusty gave me a cocky grin.

"Nothing." I was patient. "Except modern man is not self-reliant and as for making love to girls, that is only one aspect of his nature . . ."

"It's my only one. Why, just the thought of boffing some hairy boy makes me sick all over."

"Not all boys are as hairy as you," I said gaily, recklessly. Mary-Ann looked surprised while Rusty looked uneasy at this reminder of our old intimate encounter. I turned to Mary-Ann. "It's positively coquettish the way the top two buttons of his shirt are always missing."

She was relieved. "Men are so vain," she said, looking at him fondly.

"But in America only women are supposed to worry about their appearance. The real man never looks into a mirror. That's effeminate. . . ." I teased them.

"Well, *that's* changing, I guess." Mary-Ann brought Rusty's hands to her lips. "And I'm just as glad. I think men are beautiful."

"So does Rusty," I could not help but observe.

"Oh, shit, Miss Myra," was the boyish response. Soon. Soon. Soon.

BUCK LONER REPORTS —
Recording Disc No. 777 —
18 March

Flagler and Flagler have come up
with dynamite or they think its dynamite but you
never know with that woman apparently the Mon
terrey Mexican marriage certificate is a phony and
there is no record from what they can find out of
her being married down there but weve been burned
before I said to Flagler Junior who is working on
the case shell just go out and prove they lost the
records or something and then that doctor friend of
hers will swear he was a witness which is what it
sounded like on the long distance telephone call that
was bugged and what do we do then I ask you ques
tion mark well Flagler Junior seems to think they
are on solid ground with the Mexicans though he
admits that our little brown friends are not only
kind of confused in the paper works department but
if Myra thinks of it and shell think of it the bitch
they can be bribed to say that there was a marriage

when there wasnt so meanwhile I am biding my
time until tomorrow when there should be a full
final report from Mexico that there really isnt a rec
ord of this marriage in question period paragraph
Flagler Juniors New York man has already met once
with Doctor Montag and his report is on my desk
now as I dictate while being massaged by Milly who
is the best masseuse in the whole business I mean
that Milly you little angel thats right rub good and
hard it takes time but when it comes the Buck Loner
Special strike that period paragraph interesting con
versation with Letitia who thinks that Mary Ann
Pringle properly handled could make it as a record
ing star and she will make some appointments all
this is Myras doing she is meddling into everything
trying to force the kids out into the cold world when
their place is here protected and looked after I know
how well I know showbiz and all its heartbreaks and
Mary Ann will end up like all the others which is
nowhere a waitress some place assuming she doesnt
get lucky and marry some guy who will take care
of her and cherish her the way Buck Loners Acad
emy does that guy certainly wont be Rusty whos
a wild number the Sheriffs office just asked me to
keep an eye on him and I told him so yesterday told
him that he would have to watch his step or it was
the hoosegow for him he was real shook up and
asked me not to tell anybody about his scrape in
Mexico and I said nobody knows but me and Myra
who happened to be checking into his file and read
the Sheriffs last letter to me that woman is into
everything Rusty seemed upset by this I guess be
cause he thinks Myra will tell Mary Ann well its no
business of mine and thats for sure Milly you are
the best ever and if you keep that up theres a big
surprise coming your way strike that period para

graph Myra asked permission to use the infirmary
tonight God knows why I suppose she is mixing up
some poison which it is my prayer she takes Jesus
Milly dont stop Milly Jesus Milly

28

I am sitting in the infirmary, a small antiseptic white room with glass cabinets containing all sorts of drugs and wicked-looking instruments. Against one wall is an examination table which can be raised or lowered. It is now some four feet above the floor and tilted at a slight angle. Next to it are scales and measuring instruments for both height and body width. I am seated at a small surgical table, making notes while I wait for Rusty.

It is ten o'clock at night. The Academy building is dark. The students are gone. No one will disturb us. I am astonished at my own calm. All of my life's hunger is about to be fed. I am as serene as a great surgeon preparing to make the necessary incision that will root out the problem.

This morning, after Posture class, I took Rusty to one side. He has been friendly and smiling ever since our dinner at the Cock and Bull and now treats me in the confi-

dent condescending way that the ordinary young man
treats an ordinary girl.

I put a stop to that. His grinning face went pale when I
said coldly, "There's been no improvement, Rusty.
None at all. You're not trying to walk straight."

"Honest to God I am, Miss Myra, why I even practiced last night with Mary-Ann, she'll tell you I did. I
really am trying." He seemed genuinely hurt that I had
not recognized his effort.

I was somewhat kinder in my manner, sharp but in the
Eve Arden way. "I'm sure you have tried. But you need
special attention and I think I can give it. I'll expect you
at the infirmary at ten o'clock tonight."

"The infirmary?" He looked almost as puzzled as
James Craig in the sixth reel of *Kismet*.

"I've arranged everything with Uncle Buck. He agrees
with me that you need extra help."

"But what *kind* of help?" He was still puzzled but, as
yet, unsuspicious.

"You'll see." I started to go.

He stopped me. "Look, I've got a date with Mary-Ann
for dinner."

"Postpone it. You see her every night *after* dinner
anyway."

"Well, yes. But we were invited some place at ten."

"Then go at eleven. I'm sorry. But this is more important than your social life. After all, you want to be a star,
don't you?"

That was always the clincher in dealing with any of
the students. They have been conditioned from childhood in the knowledge that to achieve stardom they

might be called upon to do *anything,* and of course they would do anything because stardom is everything and worth any humiliation or anguish. So the saints must have felt in the days of Christendom, as they burned to death with their eyes on heaven where the true stars shine.

I spent all afternoon making my preparations. I have the entire procedure worked out to the last detail. When I have finished, I shall have achieved in life every dream and

29

I must write it all down now. Exactly as it happened. While it is fresh in my memory. But my hand trembles. Why? Twice I've dropped the yellow ballpoint pen. Now I sit at the surgical table, making the greatest effort to calm myself, to put it all down not only for its own sake but also for you, Randolph, who never dreamed that anyone could ever act out *totally* his fantasies and survive. Certainly your own guilty longing to kill the nerve in each of Lyndon Johnson's twenty-odd teeth *without* the use of anesthetic can never in this life be achieved, and so your dreams must feed upon pale surrogates while mine have been made reality.

Shortly after ten, Rusty arrived. He wore the usual checked shirt with two buttons missing and no T-shirt, as well as chino trousers and highly polished cowboy boots. He looked about the infirmary curiously. "I never been in here before."

"That explains why there's no physical record of you."

"Never been sick a day in my life." Oh, he was proud! No doubt of that.

"But even so, the Academy requires a record. It's one of Uncle Buck's rules."

"Yeah. I know. And I've been meaning to drop in sometime and see the Doc."

"Perhaps that won't be necessary." I placed the physical examination chart squarely in the middle of the surgical table. "Sit down." I was pleasant. He sat in a chair so close to mine that our knees touched. Quickly he swung his legs wide so that my knees were now between his and there was no possibility of further contact. It was plain that in no way do I attract him.

We chatted a moment about Mary-Ann, and about Letitia's interest in her career. I could see that Rusty was both pleased and envious, a normal reaction. Then, delicately, I got around to the subject of Mexico; he became visibly nervous. Finally, I told him that I knew what had happened.

"You won't tell Mary-Ann, will you?" That was his first response. "It would just kill her."

"Of course I won't. And of course I'll give a good report to Mr. Martinson, your parole officer."

He was startled. "You know him?"

"Oh, yes," I lied — actually I happened to come across a letter from him to Buck. "In fact, he's asked me to keep an eye on you, and I said I would."

"I hope you tell him that I sure as hell am reformed." He was vehement.

"I will — if you really are, and behave yourself, and let me try to help you with your problem."

"Of course I will, Miss Myra. You know that." He looked entirely sincere, blue eyes round as a boy's. Perhaps he is an actor after all.

"Now then, about your back. I've talked to the chiropractor who will arrange for a special brace. He couldn't be here tonight but he asked me to take an exact tracing of your spine and then he'll know what to do. So now if you'll just slip off that shirt, we'll get to work."

Resignedly, he got to his feet. Automatically his hands went to his belt buckle in order to loosen it but then, obviously recalling our last encounter, he left the belt as it was, pulling off the shirt with a certain arrogant ease.

The belt just covered his navel; otherwise he was in exactly the same state as he had been at the beginning of our first session. I was pleased that my visual recollection of him was so precise. I remembered in exact detail the tracery design of bronze hair across the pale chest, as well as the small roselike inverted nipples.

"Stand on the scales, please." I imitated the chilliest of trained nurses. "Face to the wall and we'll measure you." He put one foot on the scales, when I stopped him. "Take off those atrocious cowboy boots! They'll break the machine."

"Oh, no they won't, why . . ." He started to argue.

"Rusty!" I was sharp. "Do *exactly* as I tell you. You don't want me to tell Mr. Martinson that you've been uncooperative, do you?"

"No . . . no." Standing rest on one foot and then the

other, he awkwardly pulled off the boots. He wore
white cotton socks; one had a large hole in it through
which the big toe protruded. He grinned sheepishly.
"Guess I'm full of holes."

"That's all right." The small room was now full of the
not unpleasant odor of warm leather.

Obediently he got onto the scales exactly as I directed,
face to the wall. In a most professional way, I measured
the width of the chest, and then allowed myself the
pleasure of running my hand down the smooth warm
back, tracing the spine's curve right to the point where it
vanished, frustratingly, into the white chinos as they
swelled just below my hand, masking those famous invio-
late buttocks.

"All right," I said, marking down figures on the physical examination chart. "Now we need your weight
which is one seventy-four and your height which is six
one and a quarter. The chart's filling up nicely. All right,
you can get down."

He stepped off the scales. He was surprisingly at ease:
obviously our dinner at the Cock and Bull had given him
confidence. "This doctor can really fix me with something that will work?" He was genuinely curious.

"He thinks he can, yes. Of course, he'll have to fit you
himself. This is just the preliminary examination which,
while we're at it, Uncle Buck said I should turn into an
ordinary physical and so kill two birds with one stone, as
he put it in his colorful way."

"You mean like height and weight and that stuff?" As
yet he showed no particular alarm.

"Exactly," I said, ready now to begin to shake his self-confidence. I took a small bottle. "That means a urine specimen."

The look of surprise was exquisite as he took the bottle. "Go behind that screen." I indicated a white screen in one corner of the room.

"But . . ." he began.

"But?" I repeated pleasantly. Without a word, he went behind the screen which was waist-high. He turned and faced the wall; he fumbled with his trousers. Then there was a long moment of complete silence.

"What's the matter?" I asked.

"I . . . don't know. I guess I'm what they call pee-shy."

"Don't be. Just relax. We've got plenty of time."

The thought of "plenty of time" had a most releasing effect. Water passed into the bottle with a surging sound. He then rearranged his clothes and brought me the specimen which I took (marveling at the warmth of the glass: we are furnaces inside!) and carefully placed on it a white sticker inscribed with his name. The entire affair was conducted without a false note.

"Now then we'll just do a drawing of the spine. Loosen your belt and lie face down on the table."

For the first time he seemed aware that history might repeat itself. He stalled. "Maybe we better wait till I see the doctor."

"Rusty," I was patient but firm. "I'm just following doctor's orders and you are going to follow *my* orders, or else. Is that understood?"

"Well, yes, but . . ."

"There are no 'buts' for someone on probation."

"Yes, ma'am!" He got the point. Quickly he undid the belt buckle; then he unfastened the catch to his trousers and, holding them firmly in place, lay face-down on the table. It was a delicious sight, that slender muscular body stretched to its full length as sacrifice to some cruel goddess. His arms were at his sides, and I noticed with some amusement that he was pressing the palms hard against the table, instinctively repeating his earlier performance.

I covered his back with a large sheet of paper. Then with an eyebrow pencil, I slowly traced the spine's course from the nape of the neck to the line of his trousers.

"This is going very, very well." I sounded to my own ears exactly like Laraine Day, an all-time favorite.

"It sort of tickles," came a muffled voice. Triceps muscles writhed beneath silk-smooth skin.

"*Are* you ticklish?" This suddenly opened an unexpected vista. Fortunately my program was so designed as to include an occasional inspired improvisation.

"Well, no, not really . . ."

But I had already taken one large sweaty foot in hand (again marveling at the body heat through the thin sock) and delicately tickled the base of the toes. The effect was electric. The whole body gave a sudden twitch. With a powerful reflex, he kicked the foot from my hand, exclaiming "Cut that out!" in a masterful voice, so entirely had he forgotten his place.

I was mild. "Do that again, Rusty, and I will punish you."

"I'm sorry, Miss Myra." He was conciliatory. He looked at me over his shoulder (the tracing paper had fallen to the floor). "I guess I'm more ticklish than I thought."

"Apparently. Or perhaps I hurt you. You don't have athlete's foot, do you?"

"Oh, no. No. Not for a long time . . . in the summer, sometimes . . ."

"We'll just take a look." With some difficulty, I slipped off the damp socks. If I were a foot-fetishist like poor Myron, I would have been in seventh heaven. As it was, what excited me was his profound embarrassment, for he has the American male's horror of smelling bad. Actually, he was relatively odorless. "You must have just had a shower," I said.

He buried his face in the table. "Yeah . . . just now." Carefully I examined each toe, holding it tight as though I feared that, at any moment, one of the little piggies might decide to run all the way home. But except for a certain rigidity of the body, he did not show, in any way, distress; not even when I examined each pink toe.

"Good," I said, putting the foot down. "You're learning control. Ticklishness is a sign of sexual fear, did you know that?"

A faint "no" from the head of the table.

"That's why I was so surprised at the way you reacted when I touched your foot. From what you said at the Cock and Bull I couldn't imagine you ever being tense with a woman."

"I guess you sort of took me by surprise," was the best that he could think to say. In his present position, he obviously did not want to be reminded of his usual cockiness.

"I'm sorry," I said, deftly sliding his trousers down to his knees.

As I had anticipated, he gave a slight gasp but made no move other than to grip with both hands the sides of the trousers in an effort to keep at least his front decently covered.

On the table before me, like some cannibal banquet, the famous buttocks curved beneath frayed Jockey shorts. Below the elastic, two round holes, like eyes, revealed fair skin. Teasingly, I put my finger in one of the holes. He winced at the touch. "Doesn't Mary-Ann ever mend your clothes?"

"She . . . can't . . . sew . . ." He sounded as if he had been running hard, and could not get his breath. But at least he had steeled himself for my next move.

The total unveiling of the buttocks was accomplished in an absolute, almost religious, silence. They were glorious. Under the direct overhead light, I was able to appreciate physical details that I had missed in the office. A tiny dark mole on one cheek. An angry red pimple just inside the crack where a hair had grown in upon itself. The iridescent quality of the skin which was covered with the most delicate pale peach fuzz, visible only in a strong light and glittering now with new sweat. I could smell his fear. It was intoxicating.

I also noted that although I had pulled the Jockey shorts down to the thighs in the back, he had craftily contrived to hold them up in front, and so his honor, he believed, was only half lost.

Intimately I passed my hand over the hard buttocks, firmly locked to all intruders, and remarked, according to plan, "You aren't feverish, are you?"

"No . . . I'm O.K. . . ." The voice was barely audible. With my free hand I felt his brow; it was bathed in perspiration.

"You *are* hot. We'd better take your temperature. Besides, they want it for the chart."

As I went over to the surgical table and prepared the thermometer, he watched me dully, like a trapped animal. Then I returned to my quarry and, putting one hand on each cheek at the exact point where buttock joins thigh, I said, "Relax now."

He raised up on his arms and looked around at me, eyes suddenly bright with alarm. "*What?*"

"I've got to take your temperature, Rusty."

"But . . . *there?*" His voice broke like a teenage boy's.

"Of course. Now then . . ."

"But why can't you use the other kind, you know, in the mouth . . ." With the back of my left hand, I struck him hard across the bottom. He gasped, pulled back.

"There is more where that came from," I said coldly, noting with pleasure a certain darkening of skin where the blood had been brought to the surface by the force of my blow.

"Yes, ma'am." Defeated, the head returned to its position on the table and once again I put my hands on those firm cheeks.

"Now," I said, "relax the muscle." I could feel beneath my fingers the muscles slowly, reluctantly go slack.

I confess I was now trembling with excitement. Gently, carefully I pushed the cheeks apart until everything — secret sphincter and all — was revealed.

Normally at moments of great victory, there is a sense of letdown. But not in this case. For one thing I had half feared to find him not clean — unlike so many anal erotics I am not at all attracted by fecal matter, quite the reverse in fact. Yet had he *not* been tidy, his humiliation would have been total. So I was torn between conflicting desires. As it turned out, his shower had been thorough. The sphincter resembled a tiny pale pink tea rose, or perhaps a kitten's nose and mouth. From its circumference, like the rays of a sunburst, bronze hairs reflected the overhead light. The only disappointment was that he had craftily managed to arrange his scrotum so that it was entirely out of view, only a thick tuft of hair at the juncture of the groin indicating the direction in which it could be found. But sufficient to the moment are the revelations thereof.

I squeezed some lubricant from a tube onto my index finger and then, delicately, touched the never-used entrance. A tremor went through his whole body — the term "fleshquake" occurred to me: so Atlantis must have shuddered before the fall! Carefully, daintily, I applied the lubricant to the silky puckered surface. He held himself quite rigid, again not breathing.

Then I grew bolder. I inserted my finger into the tight hot place as far as it would go. I must have touched the prostate for he suddenly groaned, but said nothing. Then, either deliberately or through uncontrollable reflex, he brought the full force of his youthful muscularity to bear on the sphincter muscle and for a moment it felt as though my finger might be nipped off.

With my free hand, I slapped his right buttock smartly. "Relax!" I commanded. He mumbled something I could not hear and the sphincter again loosened. I then removed my finger and inserted the thermometer, after first teasing the virginal orifice with delicate probes that made him squirm. Once the thermometer was in, it was completely lost to sight for his buttocks are deep and since the legs were only slightly spread, his cheeks promptly came together when I let them go.

I then took up the chart and read off a list of childhood diseases. Chicken pox, measles, whooping cough . . . and he whispered "yes" or "no" or "I don't remember" in response to the catechism. When I was finished, I said, "All in all, a healthy young boy." My cold cheery manner was calculated to increase his alarm; obviously it did for not once would he look at me, preferring to stare at the wall just opposite, chin pushed hard against the table.

"Now let's see what's cooking." I pushed open the cheeks and slowly removed the thermometer. He was normal of course but I saw fit to lie: "Just as I thought, you do have a touch of fever. Well, we'll soon take care of that. Now roll over on your back."

He did as he was told, swiftly pulling up trousers and shorts in front; nevertheless, the line of his belt was two inches below the navel and could not, in his present position, be pulled higher. As a result, the timberline of pubic hair was briefly revealed, briefly because he promptly placed both hands over himself in an attempt to hide the quarry from the hunter's approach.

On his back, bare feet pointed and chest streaked with sweat, he seemed smaller than in fact he was, already more boy than man, despite the mature muscularity of the torso. The process of diminishing was well begun. He looked up at me, apprehensively. "Is there much more I got to do?"

"We must both follow the chart." I was enigmatic as I picked up a wooden tongue depressor. "Open your mouth." He obeyed. I pressed down the pink tongue until he gagged, noting, as I did, the whiteness of the teeth and the abnormal salivation that fear sometimes creates. "You take good care of your teeth." I gave him the sort of grudging compliment the stern nurse gives a child. "Your body, too. I was happily surprised to find that you were clean in places most boys your age neglect." Carefully I was reducing his status from man to boy to child to — ah, the triumph! He responded numbly to the progression, blinking with embarrassment.

"Now put your hands behind your head." Slowly he obeyed, aware that I could now see at least a quarter of an inch of dark pubic hair, surprisingly thick and in texture coarser than the fine hairs on the rest of his body. A pulse just above the navel beat rapidly, causing the entire stomach to quiver like some frightened small beast.

I let my hand rest lightly on his navel. Crisp hairs tickled my palm as I in turn tickled them. I could feel the pounding of the blood in his arteries. The sense of power was overwhelming. I felt as if, in some way, it was I who controlled the coursing of the blood in his veins and that it was at *my* command that the heart beat at all. I felt that I could do anything.

"You seem nervous, Rusty." I challenged him.

He swallowed hard. "No . . . no, Miss Myra. No, I'm not really. It's just that it's kind of hot in here . . ."

"And you're not enjoying your examination."

"Well, it's kind of strange, you know. . . ." His voice trailed off nervously.

"*What's* kind of strange?"

"Well, you know . . . I mean having a girl . . . you know, a lady, like you, do all this to a guy."

"Haven't you ever been examined by a nurse?"

"Never!" This reversion to the old masculine Rusty was promptly quelled by the sudden tug I gave to his Jockey shorts; the full bush was now visible, though nothing else for the shorts were stopped at the crucial juncture by the weight of his body.

With great thoroughness, I felt the different sections of his belly, taking pleasure in the firmness of muscles, hard rubber beneath silk. I lingered for quite some time over the pubic area, taking the powerful pulse of each of the two arteries that meet at the groin. I could not, however, make out even the base of his penis.

I then took an instrument which resembled sugar tongs, used to test the thickness of the skin's subcutaneous layer. With frightened eyes, he watched as I picked away at the skin of his belly, pulling the skin as high as I could and then releasing it with a snap. "Nicely resilient," I said, pinching hard as I could a fold of his belly and causing him to cry out plaintively, "Hey, that hurts!" The return to childhood was well underway.

"Stop being such a baby!" Delicately I took one of his

nipples in the tongs. He shrank from me, but the tongs pursued. I was careful, however, not to hurt him.

With feather touch, I teased the tiny inverted nipple, making him writhe at the tickling pleasure it gave him. Then, suddenly, the nipple was erect. I then teased the other nipple, manipulating the golden aureole of hairs until it, too, ceased to be concave. A glassy look came into his eyes; for the first time an erogenous zone had been explored and exploited (I do not count the probing of his sphincter which, in the context of my investigation, did not arouse him, rather the reverse). I looked at the front of his trousers to see if there was any sudden swelling but I could detect nothing.

"You had better slip off those trousers," I said. "They're getting badly creased, the way you're sweating."

"Oh, that's O.K." His voice cracked again.

"Hurry up! We haven't got all night." Grimly he sat up and pulled his trousers down over his knees. I pulled them over his feet and carefully hung them on a chair.

When I turned back to my victim, I was surprised to find him sitting up on the table, poised for flight. He had trickily used the turning of my back to restore his shorts to their normal position. Sitting as he was, bare legs dangling over the table, I could see nothing of the crotch, concealed by muscular thighs pressed close together while both hands rested protectively in his lap. He was not going to surrender the last bastion without a struggle.

"I didn't tell you to sit up, did I?" I was cold.

"But I thought you were through with me here." The

timbre of the voice had become light; he sounded like a pubescent boy trying to escape punishment.

"You're not finished until I say you are. All right. Stand up. Over here. In front of me."

He got to his feet and approached to within a foot of me. There he stood, awkwardly, hands crossed in front of him, torso glittering with sweat, legs as well proportioned as the rest of him, though somewhat overdeveloped in the thighs, no doubt the result of playing football. He was so close to me that I could feel the heat of his flesh and smell the healthy earthlike aroma the young male body exudes.

"Rest your arms at your sides and at least *try* to stand straight." He obeyed. The target was now directly in front of me, seated in front of him, at eye level. As I stared straight at the hidden area, he clenched his fists nervously, and shifted from foot to foot. The frayed Jockey shorts were unfortunately too loose to reveal more than a large rounded area, without clear definition; they were, however, splotched with fresh urine.

"Look! You wet yourself!" I pinched the damp cloth, careful to touch nothing beneath.

He gave a start. "I guess I did. I was in a hurry."

"Boys are so careless about those things." We had gone from bowel-training to bed-wetting: such was progress! I looked at the examination card. "Oh yes! Have you ever had a venereal disease?"

"Oh, no, ma'am. Never!"

"I hope you're telling me the truth." I was ominous as I wrote "no" on the chart. "We have ways of finding out, you know."

"Honest I never have. I always been careful . . . always."

"Always? Just exactly *when* did you begin with girls?"

"When?" He looked at me dumbly.

"How old were you?"

"Thirteen, I guess. I don't remember."

"Was she older than you?"

He nodded. "In high school. She was a Protestant," he added wildly.

"Did she make the advances?"

"Yes. Kind of. She'd show me hers if I showed her mine. You know, kid stuff."

"And you liked what you saw?"

"Oh, yes." A smile flickered for an instant across the frightened face.

"Did she like what she saw?"

The smile went, as he was reminded of his situation. "Well, there was no complaints."

"Would you say that you were well developed for your age?"

"I guess so. I don't know."

"Did you masturbate often?"

The face went red. "Well . . . maybe some. I guess all guys do."

"What about now?"

"Now? Oh, no. Why should I?"

"You mean Mary-Ann is quite enough to satisfy you?"

"Yes. And I don't cheat on her."

"How often do you come with her in a night?"

He gulped. "That's awful personal . . ."

I took the measuring stick and with a great cracking sound struck his right thigh. He yelled. Fear and reproach in his face, as he rubbed the hurt skin.

"There's more where that came from if you don't answer my questions."

He accepted defeat. "I guess I can go four or five times but mostly we just go a couple times because, you see, we have to get up so early . . ."

"Then you *are* quite a stud, as they say out here."

"Oh, I don't know . . ." He gestured helplessly.

"Would you say that your penis was larger than most boys' your age or smaller?"

He began to tremble, aware of the prey I was stalking. "Christ, I don't know. I mean *how* could I know?"

"You see the other boys in the shower, and you were an athlete, after all."

"I guess I didn't look . . ."

"But surely you must occasionally have taken a peep." I looked straight at the worn cotton which hid the subject of my inquiry. Both of his hands twitched, as though he wanted to protect himself.

"I guess I'm average. I never thought about it . . . honest." This of course was a lie since in every known society the adolescent male spends a great deal of time worriedly comparing himself with other males.

"You're unusually modest." I was dry. "Now I am supposed to check you for hernia. So if you'll just pull down those shorts . . ."

"But I don't have hernia," he gabbled. "I was all

checked out by this prison doctor in Mexico, and he said I was just fine in that department."

"But it does no harm to double-check. So if you'll slip them down . . ."

"Honest, I'm O.K." He was sweating heavily.

"Rusty, I get the impression that for some mysterious reason you don't want me to examine your genitals. Exactly what mischief are you trying to hide from me?"

"Nothing, honest! I got nothing to hide . . ."

"Then why are you so afraid to let me examine you?"

"Because — well, you're a woman and I'm a man . . ."

"A boy, technically . . ."

"A boy, O.K., and, well, it's just wrong."

"Then you're shy."

"Sure, I'm shy about *that*, in front of a lady."

"But surely you aren't shy with all those girls you've — what's that word of yours? — 'boffed'?"

"But that's different, when you're *both* making love, that's O.K."

"Baffling," I said. I frowned as though trying to find some way out of our dilemma. "Naturally, I want to respect your modesty. At the same time I must complete the examination." I paused; then I gave the appearance of having reached a decision. "All right. You won't have to remove your shorts . . ."

He gave a sigh of relief . . . too soon.

"However, I shall have to insert my hand inside the shorts and press each testicle as required by the chart."

"Oh." Dismay and defeat.

"I think you'll agree that's a statesmanlike compromise." On that bright note, I slid my left hand up the inside of his left thigh. He wriggled involuntarily as I forced my fingers past the leg opening of the shorts. The scrotum's heat was far greater than that of the thigh, I noticed, and the hairs were soaked with sweat.

Carefully I took his left testicle in my hand. It was unusually large and firm to the touch, though somewhat loose in the sac, no doubt due to his overheated condition. Delicately I fingered the beloved enemy, at last in my power. Then I looked up and saw that Rusty's eyes were screwed shut, as though anticipating pain. I gave it to him. I maneuvered the testicle back and forth until I had found the hole from which, in boyhood, it had so hopefully descended. I shoved it back up into the hole. He groaned. Then he gagged as I held it in place. With the gagging, I could feel the entire scrotum contract like a terrified beast, seeking escape. When he gagged again and seemed on the verge of actually being sick, I let the testicle fall back into its normal place and took my hand away.

"Jesus," he whispered. "I almost threw up."

"I'm sorry. But I have to be thorough. I'll be gentler this time." Again my hand pushed past the damp cloth and seized the right testicle, which was somewhat smaller than the left. As I maneuvered it gently about, my forefinger strayed and struck the side of something thick and smooth, rooted in wiry hair. He shuddered, but continued to suffer at my hands. I slipped the right testicle into its ancient place and held it there until I sensed he was about to gag. Then I let it drop and removed my hand.

He gave a deep sigh. "I guess that's it."

"Yes, I think so." I pretended to examine the chart.

With a sigh, he sat down on the chair opposite me and clumsily pulled on one sock, tearing the flimsy material; the toes went through the tip.

"You're very clumsy." I observed.

"Yes, ma'am." He agreed, quickly pulling on the other sock, not wanting in any way to cross me, so eager was he to escape.

"Oh, here's a question we forgot." I was incredibly sunny. "Have you been circumcised?"

The foot he was holding on his knee slid to the floor. Quickly he pressed his thighs together, wadded up his shirt, and covered the beleaguered lap. "Why, no, ma'am. I never was."

"So few Polish boys are, I'm told." I made a check on the chart. "Does the skin pull back easily?"

"Oh, sure!" He was beet-red. "Sure. I'm O.K. Mary-Ann's waiting."

"Not so fast." I was cold. "I didn't give you permission to dress, you know."

"But I thought you were finished. . . ." The deep voice was now a whine.

"I was. But your jumping the gun like that makes me very suspicious."

"Suspicious?" He was bewildered.

"Yes. First, I let you talk me out of giving you the venereal disease examination, and now you're suddenly getting dressed, without permission, just when the subject once more has to do with your penis. Rusty, I am very, very suspicious."

The blue eyes filled with tears as he sensed what was approaching. "Don't be, Miss Myra. Believe me, I'm absolutely O.K. . . ."

"We have to think of Mary-Ann, too, you know. You could make her very sick just through your carelessness."

"Honest to God, I'm O.K. They even gave me the Wassermann test in the jail. . . ." He jabbered nervously.

"I'm sure they did. But what was the result?"

"Mr. Martinson will tell you. I was a hundred per cent O.K."

"But Mr. Martinson isn't here while you are, and frankly I don't see how I can omit this part of the examination. Stand up please and put down that shirt."

"Oh, come on, please don't . . ." His voice broke again, close to a sob.

"Do as I say."

On that note of icy command, he stood up slowly and like a man going to his execution — or a schoolboy to his spanking — he put down the shirt and stood dumbly facing me. "Come over here." He came to within a few inches of where I was sitting; he was so close that my knees touched the warm fur of his shins.

"Now let's see what kind of stud you really are."

"Please . . ." He whispered. "I don't want to. It isn't right."

Deliberately I took the Jockey shorts by the elastic waistband and pulled them slowly, slowly down, enjoying each station of his shame. The first glimpse was encouraging. The base of the penis sprouted from the bronze bush at an angle of almost forty-five degrees, an earnest of vitality. It was well over an inch wide, always a good sign, with one large blue vein down the center, again promising. But another three inches of slow unveiling revealed Rusty's manhood in its entirety, I slid the shorts to the floor.

When I looked up at his face, I saw that once again the eyes were shut, the lips trembling. Then I carefully examined the object of my long and arduous hunt, at last captive. A phrase of Myron's occurred to me: "all potatoes and no meat." Rusty's balls were unusually large and impressive; one lower than the other, as they hung bulllike in the rather loose scrotal sac. They were all that I could desire. The penis, on the other hand, was not a success, and I could see now why he was so reluctant to let me see just how short it is. On the other hand both base and head are uncommonly thick and, as Myron always said, thickness not length is how you gauge the size of the ultimate erection. The skin was dead white with several not undecorative veins, while the foreskin covered the entire head, meeting at the tip in an irregular rosy pucker, plainly cousin to the sphincter I had so recently probed.

"I'm afraid, Rusty, that you've been somewhat oversold on the campus. Poor Mary-Ann. That's a boy's equipment."

This had the desired effect of stinging him into a manly response. "Ain't been no complaints," he growled. But as he did, both testicles rose in their sac as though seeking an escape hatch in case of battle, while the penis betrayed him by visibly shrinking into the safety of the brush.

"Next you'll tell me that it's not the size that counts but what you do." I followed verbal insult with physical: I took the penis firmly in my hand.

He dared not move, or speak, or even cry out. The shock had reduced him exactly as planned. I had also confirmed an old theory that although the "normal" male delights in exposing himself to females who attract him he is, conversely, terrified to do so in front of those he dislikes or fears, as though any knowledge they might obtain of the center of his being will create bad magic and hence unman him. In any case, the grail was in my hand at last, smooth, warm, soft.

My joy was complete as I slid back the skin, exposing the shiny deep rose of the head which was impressively large and beautifully shaped, giving some credence to the legend that, in action, its owner (already Rusty had become a mere appendage to this reality) was a formidable lover. He was sweaty but clean (I was so close to him that I could smell the strong but not disagreeable fernlike odor of genitals). Delicately but firmly, I pressed the glans, making the phallic eye open. Not one tear was shed. "Apparently, you *are* all right," I observed as he looked down with horror at my hand which held him firmly in its grasp, the glans penis exposed like a summer rose.

"You're also clean but beyond that I'm afraid you're something of a disappointment." The penis again shrank in my hand. "But of course you're probably still growing." The humiliation was complete. There was nothing that he could say. In actual fact, the largeness of the head had already convinced me that what I said was untrue, but policy dictated that I be scornful.

"Now then, let's see how free the foreskin is." I slid the skin forward, then back. He shuddered. "Now, you do it a few times."

To his relief, I let him go. Clumsily he took himself in one hand as though never before had he touched this strange object, so beloved of Mary-Ann. He gave a few halfhearted tugs to the skin, looking for all the world like a child frightened in the act of masturbating.

"Come on," I said, "you can do better than that."

He changed his grip to the one he obviously used when alone. His hand worked rapidly as he pumped himself like one of those machines that extract oil from the earth, milk from the cow, water from shale. After several minutes of intense and rhythmic massage I noted, with some surprise, that though the head had become a bit larger and darker, the stem had not changed in size. Apparently he knew how to restrain himself. He continued for another minute or two, the only sound in the room his heavy breathing and the soft waterlike sound of skin slapping against skin; then he stopped.

"You see," he said. "It works O.K."

"But I didn't tell you to stop."

"But if I keep on . . . I mean . . . well, Christ, a man's going to . . ."

"A boy," I corrected.

"A boy's going to . . . to . . ."

"To what?"

"Get . . . excited."

"Go right ahead. I'd be amused to see what Mary-Ann sees in you."

Without another word, grimly, he set to work and continued for some time, sweating hard. But still we were denied the full glory. Some lengthening and thickening took place but not to the fullest degree.

"Is anything wrong?" I asked sweetly.

"I don't know." He gulped, trying to catch his breath. "It can't . . . won't . . ." He was incoherent at the double humiliation.

"Do you often have this problem with Mary-Ann?" I sounded as compassionate as Kay Francis, as warm as June Allyson.

"Never! I swear . . ."

"Five times in one night and now this! Really, you young boys are such liars."

"I wasn't lying. I just don't know what's wrong. . . ." He beat at himself as though through sheer force he could tap the well of generation. But it was no use. Finally I told him to stop. Then I took over, practicing a number of subtle pressures and frictions learned from Myron . . . all to no avail.

In a curious way the absence of an erection, though not part of the plan, gave me an unexpected thrill: to have so cowed my victim as to short-circuit his legendary powers as a stud was, psychologically, far more fulfilling than my original intention.

While I was vigorously shaking him, he made the long-expected move that would complete the drama, the holy passion of Myra Breckinridge.

"Do you . . ." He began tentatively, looking down at me and the loose-stemmed rose that I held in my hand.

"Do I what?"

"Do you want me to . . . well, to ball you?" The delivery was superb, as shy as a nubile boy requesting a first kiss.

I let go of him as though in horror. "Rusty! Do you know who you're talking to?"

"Yes, Miss Myra. I'm sorry. I didn't mean to offend you. . . ."

"What sort of woman do you think I am?" I took the heavy balls in my hand, like an offering. "These belong to Mary-Ann, and no one else, and if I ever catch you playing around with anybody else, I'll see that Mr. Martinson puts you away for twenty years."

He turned white. "I'm sorry. I didn't know. I thought maybe . . . the way you were . . . doing what you were doing. . . . I'm sorry, really." The voice stopped.

"You have every reason to be sorry." Again I let him go; the large balls swung back between his legs, and continued gently to sway, like a double pendulum. "In any case, if I had wanted you to — as you put it — 'ball me,' it's very plain that you couldn't. As a stud, you're a disaster."

He flushed at the insult but said nothing. I was now ready for my master stroke. "However, as a lesson, I shall ball you."

He was entirely at sea. "Ball *me?* How?"

"Put out your hands." He did so and I bound them together with surgical gauze. Not for nothing had I once been a nurses' aide.

"What're you doing that for?" Alarm growing.

With a forefinger, I flicked the scrotal sac, making him cry out from shock. "No questions, my boy." When the hands were firmly secured, I lowered the examination table until it was just two feet from the floor. "Lie down," I ordered. "On your stomach."

Mystified, he did as he was told. I then tied his bound hands to the top of the metal table. He was, as they say, entirely in my power. If I had wanted, I could have killed him. But my fantasies have never involved murder or even physical suffering for I have a horror of blood, preferring to inflict pain in more subtle ways, destroying totally, for instance, a man's idea of himself in relation to the triumphant sex.

"Now then, up on your knees."

"But . . ." A hard slap across the buttocks put an end to all objections. He pulled himself up on his knees, legs tight together and buttocks clenched shut. He resembled a pyramid whose base was his head and white-socked feet, and whose apex was his rectum. I was now ready for the final rite.

"Legs wide apart," I commanded. Reluctantly, he moved his knees apart so that they lined up with the exact edges of the table. I was now afforded my favorite view of the male, the heavy rosy scrotum dangling from the groin above which the tiny sphincter shyly twinkled in the light. Carefully I applied lubricant to the mystery that even Mary-Ann has never seen, much less violated.

"What're you doing?" The voice was light as a child's. True terror had begun.

"Now remember the secret is to relax entirely. Otherwise you could be seriously hurt."

I then pulled up my skirt to reveal, strapped to my groin, Clem's dildo which I borrowed yesterday on the pretext that I wanted it copied for a lamp base. Clem had been most amused.

Rusty cried out with alarm. "Oh, no! For God's sake, don't."

"Now you will find out what it is the girl feels when you play the man with her."

"Jesus, you'll split me!" The voice was treble with fear. As I approached him, dildo in front of me like the god Priapus personified, he tried to wrench free of his bonds, but failed. Then he did the next best thing, and brought his knees together in an attempt to deny me entrance. But it was no use. I spread him wide and put my battering ram to the gate.

For a moment I wondered if he might not be right about the splitting: the opening was the size of a dime while the dildo was over two inches wide at the head and nearly a foot long. But then I recalled how Myron used to have no trouble in accommodating objects this size or larger, and what the fragile Myron could do so could the inexperienced but sturdy Rusty.

I pushed. The pink lips opened. The tip of the head entered and stopped.

"I can't," Rusty moaned. "Honestly I can't. It's too big."

"Just relax, and you'll stretch. Don't worry."

He made whatever effort was necessary and the

pursed lips became a grin allowing the head to enter, but not without a gasp of pain and shock.

Once inside, I savored my triumph. I had avenged Myron. A lifetime of being penetrated had brought him only misery. Now, in the person of Rusty, I was able, as Woman Triumphant, to destroy the adored destroyer.

Holding tight to Rusty's slippery hips, I plunged deeper. He cried out with pain.

But I was inexorable. I pushed even farther into him, triggering the prostate gland, for when I felt between his legs, I discovered that the erection he had not been able to present me with had now, inadvertently, occurred. The size was most respectable, and hard as metal.

But when I plunged deeper, the penis went soft with pain, and he cried out again, begged me to stop, but now I was like a woman possessed, riding, riding, riding my sweating stallion into forbidden country, shouting with joy as I experienced my own sort of orgasm, oblivious to his staccato shrieks as I delved and spanned that innocent flesh. Oh, it was a holy moment! I was one with the Bacchae, with all the priestesses of the dark bloody cults, with the great goddess herself for whom Attis unmanned himself. I was the eternal feminine made flesh, the source of life and its destroyer, dealing with man as incidental toy, whose blood as well as semen is needed to make me whole!

There was blood at the end. And once my passion had spent itself, I was saddened and repelled. I had not meant actually to tear the tender flesh but apparently I had, and the withdrawing of my weapon brought with it bright blood. He did not stir as I washed him clean (like a loving mother), applying medicine to the small cut, inserting gauze (how often had I done this for Myron!). Then I unbound him.

Shakily, he stood up, rubbing tears from his swollen face. In silence he dressed while I removed the harness of the dildo and put it away in the attaché case.

Not until he was finally dressed did he speak. "Can I go now?"

"Yes. You can go now." I sat down at the surgical table and took out this notebook. He was at the door when I said, "Aren't you going to thank me for the trouble I've taken?"

He looked at me, face perfectly blank. Then, tonelessly, he murmured, "Thank you, ma'am," and went.

And so it was that Myra Breckinridge achieved one of the great victories for her sex. But one which is not yet entirely complete even though, alone of all women, I know what it is like to be a goddess enthroned, and all-powerful.

30

I sit now at the card table. Through the window I can see the turning chorus girl in front of the Château Marmont; only she is not turning. A power failure? are they making repairs? or is she at last being dismantled? The question takes on symbolic importance since she is, to me, Hollywood. She must never *not* be allowed to dominate the Strip.

Rusty did not appear at school today. I would have been disappointed if he had. But what did distress me was Mary-Ann's absence from Posture. She has never before missed one of my classes.

Discouraged and uneasy, I rang Miss Cluff to see if Mary-Ann had attended the Bell Telephone Hour class. She had not, "I haven't seen hide nor hair of her. But you know how girls are. It's probably her time. . . ." Bell-like laughter from Miss Cluff. Next I rang the girls' dormitory. The matron told me that Mary-Ann had not returned the previous evening, and she had already made a report to Buck.

I confess I was terrified. Had Rusty told her what had happened? I could not believe it. Masculine pride (no matter how damaged) would have prevented him. But he still could have told her *something* which had made her leave the school . . . and me. I had a sudden vision of them together in Mexico, growing marijuana, utterly happy. The thought was too depressing. Also, I reminded myself, impractical since he is on parole and may not leave L.A., much less cross the border.

Matters were not much helped when I received a call from Buck's office to see him at five. I found him looking altogether too pleased with himself. With him was a typical California type: a bronzed empty face with clear eyes and that vapid smile which the Pacific Ocean somehow manages to impress upon the lips of almost everyone doomed to live in any proximity to those tedious waters. It is fascinating to observe how, in a single generation, stern New England Protestants and keen New York Jews are all entirely Tahitianized by that dead ocean with its sweet miasmic climate in which thoughts become dreams while perceptions blur and distinctions are so erased that men are women are men are nothing are everything are one. Gentlemen, the desire and the pursuit of the whole ends at Santa Monica!

The typical specimen was Charlie Flagler Junior, lawyer. He gave me the whitest of smiles, the firmest of handshakes and then, at Buck's insistence, he let me have it. "Mrs. Breckinridge, as you know, in representing my client, Mr. Loner, or any client, I — we must of course try to leave no stone unturned in order to — like make it *crystal clear* what their position is."

Buck clapped his hands together, as if in applause. Then he said, "I think, Myra, you should know that Charlie's dad and me have been pals for lo! these many years, ever since he handled me when I had that big row with the Blue Network."

"I guess we value Mr. Loner's account more than almost any single noncorporate account, not only for old times' sake — like Dad says — but because Buck Loner has a *reputation* in this town" — Charlie Flagler Junior's voice became very grave and solemn — "for being like a straight-shooter."

"For Christ's sake," I said, no doubt in the same tone that Dr. Margaret Mead must have used in trying to extract a straight bit of folklore from *her* Polynesians, "stop gassing and tell me what lousy trick you're up to now."

Buck's face half shut; he looked pained. Charlie Flagler Junior gave me a curious look. I imagined him stretched out before me the way Rusty had been; a satisfying vision except, curiously enough, so complete was last night's experience that any repetition of it would be redundant, even in fantasy. I have accomplished what nature intended me to do and except for one last turn to the screw, I am complete.

"No lousy trick, Mrs. Breckinridge." The young lawyer wanted to appear grieved but the Polynesian face has only two expressions: joy and incomprehension. He looked quite stupid. "I simply must respect my client's wishes and defend his interests which in this case are your claim to like half the value of this Westwood property, due you as the alleged widow of his nephew."

"Alleged?" I was ready for battle.

Joy filled the brown Pacific face, as though a toasted breadfruit had been offered him after a long swim with Dorothy Lamour. "Alleged. The marriage certificate you gave us is an out-and-out forgery."

I was not as prepared to answer this charge as I thought I would be. The game is now becoming most tricky and dangerous. One false move and all will come to a dead halt, like the ominously stationary ten-times-life-size chorine outside my window. "Mr. Charlie Flagler Junior and you, Buck Loner, brother of Gertrude and cheerful thief, I am the heiress to half this property, and I am going to get it. So don't think for one moment you can hold out on me."

"Honey, we're not trying to keep what's yours from you." Buck was plaintive. "That's the last thing on our minds but we've got to make sure you really are entitled to it. I mean you could be some kind of impersonator, saying you are who you are."

"Gertrude gave you two hundred dollars back in Philadelphia when you were twenty years old to pay for the abortion of the daughter of the Rexall druggist you knocked up and refused to marry."

Buck turned white. The Polynesian remained brown. Buck cleared his throat, "I'm not saying you didn't know Gertrude and the boy well. Obviously you did . . ."

"The point is like this," said Charlie Flagler Junior, "you have to *prove* you were married. That's all."

"I shall prove it." I rose to go. The men rose, too, with a new respect. At least they don't underestimate their adversary. "Proof will arrive before the end of the week. Meanwhile, Uncle Buck, I shall list all the loans Gertrude made you over the years, and I shall expect repayment, with interest." I slammed the door as I left.

I have just talked to Dr. Montag in New York. He dithered. I was firm. "Randolph, you owe this to me. You owe this to Myron. I don't want to blackmail you emotionally but you also owe it to the insights we exchanged, the three of us, at the Blue Owl Grill. We made you just as you made us. Now we are at the crunch. . . ."

"The what?" His nervous wheezing often keeps him from hearing what others say.

" 'Crunch' is a word currently favored by the keener journalists. It means the showdown, the moment of truth. Well, this is the crunch, and I am appealing to you, not only as Myron's analyst and my dentist but as our only friend. Fly out here tomorrow."

"But, Myra, I can't. Your appeal reaches me at every level, there's no doubt about that. I am touched in every department from lower id, as your husband used to say, to upper superego, but there is the problem of my other patients. They need me. . . ."

"Randolph." I was peremptory. "I'll cut you in for ten per cent of the take."

There was an alarming series of wheezes and coughs at the other end of the line. Then Dr. Montag said what sounded like "Between, Myra."

"Between what?"

"Fifteen!" he shouted from the Island of Manhattan. "Fifteen per cent and I'm in L.A. tomorrow."

"Answered like a true Adlerian! *Fifteen it is!*" I knew my man. Many was the night that the three of us used to sit until the Blue Owl closed discussing Randolph's inordinate greed for pastry and money. It was — is — the most likable thing about him. With that taken care of, I can now

31

Life continues to support Myra Breckinridge in all her schemes to obtain uniqueness. As I write this, Mary-Ann is asleep in my bed (I have fixed up the daybed in here for myself). It is three in the morning. We have talked and wept together for five hours. I have never known such delight. Last night with Rusty was religious ecstasy; tonight a rebirth.

While I was writing in this notebook, there was a rap at the door. I opened it. Mary-Ann stood in the doorway, pale and bedraggled and carrying a Pan Am overnight zipper bag. "Miss Myra, I've got to talk to you. You're the only person I can." With that she burst into tears and I took her in my arms, reveling in the full rounded warmth of that body, so reminiscent of the early Lana Turner. In a curious way, though she is so much younger and more vulnerable than I, she suggests a mother figure to me, which is madness since in our relationship I am, necessarily, the one who is wise, the one who comforts and directs. I daresay my hatred of my own mother must have had some *positive* element in it since I am now able to feel genuine warmth for another woman, and a mere girl at that. I must discuss the matter thoroughly with Randolph.

Soon the sobbing ceased, and I poured her a glass of gin which she drank neat. This seemed to steady her.

"Rusty's gone again." She sat on the daybed, and blew her nose. Her legs are every bit as beautiful as Eleanor Powell's in the last reel of *Rosalie,* on those drums.

"Gone where?" I was about to say that any boy on parole is not apt to take a long trip, but I thought better of it.

"I don't know. It happened last night." She dried her eyes.

"Yes?" I was cautious. "You were with him last night?"

She nodded. "We were supposed to have dinner but he said you wanted to see him at ten. . . ."

"A routine chat." I was casual. "I'm sorry I picked such an odd hour and ruined your dinner but I was busy with Miss Cluff and . . ."

She was, happily, not interested in his visit to me. "Anyway he didn't pick me up till after eleven, and I've never seen him in such a bad mood . . ."

"Strange," I added to the official record, "he seemed quite cheerful when he left me. In fact, he thanked me profusely for the help I'd given him."

"I know you were nice to him. You always are — now. Anyway he didn't mention you. He just picked a fight with me, over nothing, and I got angry and then he said maybe I'd better go back to the dorm and not spend the night with him. He said he was . . ." she paused, tears beginning, "sick of me, sick of women, and wanted just to go off by himself. . . ."

"Sick of you or of women in general?" This was a key point.

"I don't know exactly what he said, I was so upset. Both, I guess."

Apparently I had done my work better than I expected.

"On top of that, he said he was feeling lousy and he'd pulled a muscle or something and it hurt him to sit down . . . oh, I don't know, he was just awful. But then I told him about the date I'd made for him, and that cheered him up a bit."

"What date?"

"You won't be mad at me?" She looked so frightened, young, vulnerable that I wanted to hold her in my arms. "Of course not, dear." I was Janet Gaynor. "I could never be angry with you."

"You *are* a friend." She gave me a dim watery smile. "Well, I had got us both invited to Letitia Van Allen's home at Malibu, in the Colony."

I sat up straight. *I* have never been invited to Letitia's house but then of course I have yet to be of any use to her as a purveyor of studs. Now poor Mary-Ann had fallen unwittingly into Letitia's trap. "Just how did this invitation come about?"

"Well, I was in her office and we were talking about this date she'd made for me with that record company and then, I don't know, the conversation got around to

Rusty and she asked to see a picture of him, and I showed
her the ones I always carry and she said he was very
handsome and had star quality and I asked her if she
wanted to meet him . . . oh, I know you didn't want
him to talk to her until June . . ."

"It would have been better *after* his closed-circuit TV
performance. Anyway the damage is done. So you took
him to Malibu last night."

She nodded bleakly. "There were a dozen people
there, all so successful and rich. One was a star. You
know, the one who's in that television series that was just
canceled by CBS, *Riptide?* He was nice but drunk. Anyway Letitia made a big fuss over Rusty, who was rude as
could be to her and to everybody else. I've never seen
him act like that before."

"Perhaps he had something on his mind."

"Well, whatever it is it was eating him up, for suddenly he gets up and says to Miss Van Allen. 'I got to
cut. This isn't my scene.' And left just like that, *without
me*. I was never so embarrassed and hurt. Anyway Miss
Van Allen couldn't have been nicer and said she
wouldn't hold it against Rusty and since it was so late I'd
better sleep over, which I did, though I didn't sleep
much, with that boy from *Riptide* banging on the door
all night."

I poured her more gin which she drank. Her spirits
improved. "Anyway, today I called Rusty at the place
where he's staying and they said he didn't come home
last night, and then I called the Academy and they said
he didn't go to any of his classes, and then I got scared
that maybe he was killed or something so I called the po-

lice but they didn't know anything. Then I waited in the dorm all evening for him to call and when finally he didn't, I came here. . . ." Her voice had become quavery again.

"You did the right thing," I said. "And I want you to stay here with me until everything's straightened itself out."

"You're so good, Miss Myra!"

"Not at all. Now don't worry about Rusty. Nothing's happened to him. He's probably in a bad mood because of the situation he's in." Then I told her in detail about Rusty's Mexican adventures. "So you see he's on parole and that means the probation officer must always know where he is. So if Rusty ever really did disappear, Uncle Buck and I would be the first to know about it."

Mary-Ann frowned, still absorbing what I had told her. I gave her more gin which she drank as though it was her favorite drink, Seven-Up. "He promised me he was never going to see any of those boys he used to hang out with."

"Well, he's young. Let him have his fun. As long as he stays out of jail, of course."

She shook her head, suddenly grim. "It's them or me, I told him."

"And of course it will be you." I was soothing as I began to spread and arrange my net. "Don't worry. Now lie down and rest while we chat."

She gave me a grateful smile and stretched out on the daybed. It was all I could do not to sit beside her and caress those extraordinary breasts, made doubly attrac-

tive for me since they are Rusty's to do with as he likes,
or so he believes. Having raped his manhood, I shall now
seduce his girl. Beyond that, ambition stops and godhood
begins.

We talked of everything. She is totally in love with
Rusty, though shaken by what has happened as well as
by my revelation of his Mexican capers. She has had only
three lovers in her life, all male. Lesbianism is repulsive to
her. But she did agree, after the fourth glass of gin, that
she felt entirely secure and warm with me, and that one
woman could offer another, under the right circumstances, great reassurance and affection.

Finally, slightly drunk, I took her into the bedroom
and helped her to undress. The breasts are *better* than
Lana Turner's in *They Won't Forget*. Smooth and white
with large rosy nipples (in a curious way they are an ex-
aggerated version of Rusty's own), their shape is marvelously subtle . . . at least what I could see of them, for
she promptly pulled on her nightdress and only then removed her panties, hiding from me that center of Rusty's
sexual being in which he has so many times (but never
again if I can help it!) spent himself.

The thought that soon I shall know intimately the
body he knew so made me tremble that I did not dare
embrace her good night but instead blew her a kiss from
the door, shut it, and promptly rang Mr. Martinson, who
was angry at being waked up. But he did tell me that
Rusty had decided to leave the Academy and take a permanent job with a firm that sells foreign cars on Melrose
Avenue; however, when I asked where Rusty was stay-

ing, Mr. Martinson told me that it was none of my business. Needless to say, I told him where and how to head in, and hung up.

Now I must find some way of breaking the news to Mary-Ann. This will be tricky because under no circumstances must they be allowed to resume their love affair. That is at an end.

A miraculous omen! I just looked out the window at the enormous woman and she is again turning gaily upon her axis, beautiful and omnipotent, the very image of deity!

32

Dr. Montag is sitting on the daybed reading my description of the conquest of Rusty. I sit at the card table, writing these lines, waiting for his comment. Tomorrow we meet Buck and his lawyers. The showdown.

Randolph is wheezing through clouds of pipe smoke. He is frowning. I suppose he disapproves. Yet of all people he should understand what it is that I have done. He looks simply God-awful. He thinks he's in Hawaii. He is wearing a flowered short-sleeved shirt that hangs outside his shiny black rabbinical trousers and

33

Randolph has returned to his motel for a nap; he is still not used to the change in time and wants to be at his best for tomorrow's meeting. We have prepared two lines of attack; at the worst, one will succeed.

The description of my life's triumph did not entirely please him which, naturally, does not please *me*, and that is what matters.

"Am I to understand all this really happened?" Ashes fell upon the page which I snatched from his hand. Randolph's pipe often produces cinders as well as smoke, for he has a tendency to blow through the stem when ill at ease.

"Exactly," I said. "At least you'll have to agree that I've got him down in black and white, once and for all, every detail, every hair, every pimple."

"You've got his *outside*, yes." Judiciously he arranged

a screen of smoke between us. "But that's just Rusty's skin, you haven't shown his inside."

"I haven't shown his inside, dear Randolph, because I don't know it. And, if I may say so, it is presumptuous for anyone to even pretend he can know what another person's interior is really like, short of an autopsy. The only thing we can ever know for certain is skin, and I now know his better than he does himself."

"Possibly. Possibly." Randolph still appeared distressed.

"In fact," I improvised, "nothing matters except what is visible to the eye. For me to write, as I shall when you go, that you *looked* distressed at this moment could very easily be a projection on my part, and misreading of your mood. To be accurate, I should simply write that while you were reading my notes there was a double crease between your brows, which is not usual, since . . ."

"It is *not* a projection to say that I am distressed. And up to a point we can, more or less, assume that we know what others are feeling, at least at the more accessible levels of consciousness. At this moment, I am feeling a certain distress for that young man, a certain male empathy. After all, it is a most unpleasant thing to be assaulted anally and I think we can both assume that he was not happy, no matter how mute the skin."

"I agree and that's why in my review of what happened, I not only recorded his conversation but tried to give what I believed were his feelings when he spoke. Yet I realize that at best my interpretation is entirely subjective, and perhaps false. Since I wanted to frighten and humiliate him, I chose to regard his groans and grunts as symptoms of fright and humiliation."

"Which, no doubt, they were. Although we must never rule out the possibility that he was enjoying himself."

"If that is true, my life's work has failed." I was very grave. I have never been more serious.

"Or succeeded in ways you do not yet understand. In any case, his girlfriend is living with you, isn't she?"

"Yes, she came to me. Of all the people she knows, I am the one she turned to. The irony is perfect." So is my delight!

"Does she know what you've done?"

"Of course not."

"What will happen if she finds out?"

"I have no intention of telling her. As for Rusty, I don't think either of us needs a degree in psychiatry" (Randolph looked momentarily unhappy; he has only an M.A. in psychology) "to know that he will never tell anyone what was done to him."

"Perhaps not." Randolph's pipe went off again. One bright cinder burned a hole in the carpet. "But aren't you afraid he may want compensation for what you did, particularly if he is as healthy and 'normal' as you think?"

"What sort of compensation?"

"He might take *physical* revenge on you. Do to you what you did to him."

"Rape? Not very likely. He's much too terrified. No, I've heard the last of him, except in connection with Mary-Ann . . ."

Randolph listened carefully as I told him how I

planned, with every appearance of love and affection, to possess Mary-Ann in order that the cycle be completed.

"What cycle?"

"The justification of Myron's life." I was prompt. I have intellectualized everything, as I always do, to the despair of Randolph, who is, despite all his modish pretensions and quibbling subterfuges, entirely emotional, in many ways a dead ringer for Jean Hersholt. "By acting out what was done to him, I exalt him — the idea of him, anyway — and also avenge him . . ."

"*Avenge* him? In what way? The Myron I knew was hardly a victim. Rather the contrary."

"No, he was victim. I know that now. But no matter what he really was . . ."

"A marvelous man . . ."

"How you enjoy throwing that in my face!" I was stung and deeply hurt, as I always am, by reminders that Randolph worshipped Myron and cannot, at heart, bear me.

"Now, now you must not project. When I praise Myron, I praise *him*. I don't denigrate you."

"*You* are the one projecting now. But, in any case, once I have completed my seduction, I shall be free of all guilt toward Myron and for Myron. I shall be a new woman, literally new, something unique under the sun."

"But who and what will you be?"

I answered vehemently, at length, but said nothing, for, as usual, Randolph, in his blundering way, has touched upon the dilemma's horn: I have no clear idea as to my ultimate identity once every fantasy has been acted out with living flesh. All that I do know is that I

shall be freed of obsession and, in this at least, be like no
one else who ever lived.

Randolph then departed for his nap to be followed by
a trip to Disneyland. So here I sit, making these notes.
Suddenly ill at ease. Why? The telephone rings

34

That was Letitia. She came straight to the point. "Rusty's living with me. He's down at the beach house right now."

"Letitia!" That was the best I could do. Not even in my wildest dreams had I ever connected the two of them, particularly after Mary-Ann's description of Rusty's rudeness to Letitia on the famous night.

"All I can say, Myra, is you sure know how to pick 'em. That is the best Grade A stud I have ever had and as, rumor hath doubtless had it here at the heart of the Industry, Letitia Van Allen has made many a trip to the old corral."

I could think of nothing but Rusty's soft rose wobbling childishly in my hand. "Is he really the *very* best stud of all?"

"The very best, and I've you to thank for it. When I saw how you had conned that girlfriend of his into bringing him to my house, I said to myself: Myra Breck-inridge is a *pal!*"

I was startled but delighted at being given full credit for maneuvering Rusty into Letitia's orbit. "Of course I knew you'd enjoy meeting him." I was neutral, not want-ing to betray the fact that it was Mary-Ann I had wanted Letitia to help, not Rusty.

"He's *everything* I like!" Letitia roared into the tele-phone. "In fact, the moment I clapped eyes on him, I said, 'God, Letitia, but that's it!' "

"But Mary-Ann told me he behaved abominably at your house."

"Natch! That's what I like. He was sullen, sneering, raging inside . . ."

"I'm sure he was." I purred with secret satisfaction.

"But I knew by the way that he insulted everybody and stormed out of the house that I'd soon be seeing him again. And I did. The next day he came to the office and apologized, still sullen, of course, but wanting to make up . . . said he'd had a fight with the girl, as if I didn't know, and could I get him work. So I said you bet I can, and signed him to a five-year representational talent con-tract. Then I rang up Maddox Motors and got him a job as a mechanic. He was grateful, and showed it, right then and there, on the old four-poster. That chenille bed-spread will never be the same again."

"And it was really marvelous?" I was genuinely curi-ous to see how Rusty would perform after my discipli-nary session.

"I thought, Myra," Letitia's words were measured and awed, "that he would *kill* me. I have never known anyone so masterful. He threw me on the bed and struck me repeatedly. Yes, *struck* Letitia Van Allen who *never* goes that route but did this time. I'm still black and blue and totally happy, all thanks to you!"

"You exaggerate." Rusty's compensation with Letitia for what he had suffered at my hands will fascinate Randolph. "But did he . . . well, say anything about leaving school, about me?"

"Not a word, except that he was sick of being treated like a kid and wanted to get to work. He won't talk about you at all. Did you ever lay him?"

"Not in any classic way, no. But what does he say about Mary-Ann?"

"That's why I'm calling you. He feels guilty. I can tell. Now, let's put our cards on the table. I want him all to myself as long as possible which won't be very long, since once he starts making a living he'll be off with the cute young chicks, leaving poor old Letitia to her Scotch and casting couch. But for now I'm hanging on to him for dear life. So what do we do to keep Miss Pieface out of our lives?"

I told her exactly how it could be done . . . and will be done tonight! Thanking me profusely, and vowing eternal friendship, Letitia hung up.

35

Three in the morning again. Joy and despair, equally mixed, as I watch, hypnotized, the turning statue, and think for the first time how lonely she must be out there, ten times life-size, worshipped but not loved, like me.

As soon as Mary-Ann returned from school, I suggested that we drive down to the beach in my rented Chrysler and watch the sunset. She seemed to like the idea. Though she was plainly fretting over Rusty, she did not mention him once, as we drove along the Pacific Highway, bumper to bumper with the rush-hour crowd as it crawled slowly between the dull sea and the brown crumbly hills of fine shifting dust, forever dropping houses into the sea. This coastal region is quite inhospitable to man. What we have done is colonize the moon, and so are lunatic.

To amuse Mary-Ann, I acted out the entire plot of *Marriage Is a Private Affair*. She was very much amused, particularly when I quoted Parker Tyler to her. We both agreed that his explication of that paradigmatic wartime film is altogether wonderful.

Just as the red-smog was vanishing into the olive-drab sea, I turned casually into the private road of the Malibu Beach Colony, a number of opulent beach houses jammed together between road and sea; many are occupied by stars of the first and current (if that is not a contradiction!) magnitude.

"But this is where Miss Van Allen lives!" Until then, Mary-Ann had been indifferent to her surroundings, doubtless conducting some inner dialogue with Rusty even as I spoke of James Craig and the great days.

"Really? Where?" In fact, I did not know which was Letitia's house, Mary-Ann indicated a gray clapboard Provincetown-style house. "Then why don't we drop in and say hello?"

"Oh, no! I couldn't. Not after last time. Not after the way Rusty talked to her. I'd be too uncomfortable."

"Nonsense." I parked in front of the darkened house. The light from the sea was now very faint. "I'm sure she's forgiven him. She's used to artistic temperament. After all, that's her business."

"But he was so awful, and I looked so silly."

"Don't be a goose!" I took her hand and led her to the door and rang the bell. "Besides, this will be good for your career." To this argument, the only response was acquiescence.

From inside the house I could hear a Benny Goodman record (Letitia belongs in fact to the generation to which I belong in spirit). No one, however, answered the doorbell.

"She's out." Mary-Ann was relieved. "Let's go."

"But I hear music. Come on." I opened the front door and led the reluctant Mary-Ann into a large darkened room that looked onto the sea. Silhouetted against the last light of the day, two figures were dancing, intertwined.

According to plan, I switched on the light. Rusty and Letitia leapt apart; they wore bathing suits (marvelously reminiscent of Garfield and Crawford in *Humoresque*).

"What the hell!' exclaimed Letitia, simulating anger.

"Darling, I couldn't be sorrier!" I simulated alarm.

Both Rusty and Mary-Ann were genuinely shocked; but where she was hurt, he was truculent.

It was Mary-Ann who made the first move. "Where," she asked him in a quavering voice, "have you been?"

But Letitia did not allow him to answer. "Come on, children, let's all have a nice drink!" She crossed to the sanctuary of the bar at the end of the room opposite the plate-glass window, black now from the light within.

Rusty simply stared at Mary-Ann. Not once did he look at me.

". . . Then," said Letitia comfortably, "we can sit down and discuss this like adults." (Greer and Joan in *When Ladies Meet*). "Who wants what?" But no one answered her.

Then Mary-Ann repeated, "Where have you been all this time?"

To which Rusty responded in a clear hard voice, "What are you doing with *her?*" And he gave me a look of perfect hate.

"Myra's my friend." Mary-Ann's voice was faint.

Letitia gargled some Scotch and then said hoarsely, "Rusty's been staying here while I get him launched over at Fox with this new series. You sure you don't want a drink, honey? Or you, Myra?"

"Are you *living* with this woman?" Mary-Ann was still unable to comprehend the situation.

"Now, dear, don't get upset." Letitia was soothing. "Rusty and I do have a great deal in common but neither one of us would want to hurt you for the world." She gave Rusty a shot of whiskey which he gulped, eyes still on Mary-Ann. "In fact, he was all for telling you this morning but I thought we should wait. Anyway now that the cat's out of the bag . . ."

"It's all my fault, Letitia." I was humble. "The whole thing."

"No, dear. Don't blame yourself. It's probably for the best. Personally I like everything in the open. That's the way I am. And that's why I'm here to tell all the world that I'm proud to be in love with Rusty, and proud that he loves me!"

With a wail, Mary-Ann fled back to the car. When Rusty started to follow her, Letitia's arm darted out and held him back. "She'll be all right. She's got Myra." That stopped the young man. He made no further move to follow the girl.

Then Letitia crossed to me. She was thrilling, every inch of her a great actress on the order of Frances Dee or Ann Dvorak. She took my hands in hers and kissed my cheek. "Be kind to the girl."

"I will, Letitia. You know I will."

"When she's older, she'll understand how these things

just happen and that we are all of us simply putty in the hands of the great potter." The metaphor was mixed, but the delivery was bravura. "Rusty and I need each other. That's all there is. A man, a woman . . . What else? It's Kismet." She let go my hands. "Good night, Myra."

I said good night and followed Mary-Ann into the darkness. She was in the car, weeping. I comforted her as best I could which was hardly at all since I am a nervous driver and need both hands on the wheel when driving through traffic, particularly along Sunset Boulevard at night.

Back at the apartment, Mary-Ann recovered sufficiently to finish the bottle of gin. But her mood did not improve. She is shattered. She cannot understand why Rusty has deserted her or what he sees in Letitia. This was of course my cue to point out that for an ambitious young man like Rusty to be taken up by Letitia is a sure way to stardom.

"But he *swore* he'd never do anything like that. He's just not that kind of a boy . . ."

"Apparently he is. I mean, let's face it, he is *living* with her." Since this brought on more tears, as I intended, I took her in my arms. She wept into my neck. Never in my life have I felt so entirely warm and contented.

"Forget him," I whispered into a soft pink ear that smelled of Lux toilet soap.

Suddenly she sat up and dried her eyes. "I could murder him!" Her voice had gone cello with rage.

"Now, now you mustn't be angry with the boy." I was supremely anodyne. "After all, that's the way he is. You can't change people. Just think how lucky you are to have learned all this *now* instead of after you were married, and had children."

"I'll never marry! I hate men." She got shakily to her feet (she was quite drunk), and made her way to the bedroom.

When I helped her to undress (for once she really needed help), she was grateful for my attentions which I managed to make discreet, despite the turmoil caused in me whenever those marvelous breasts are unveiled. Then she threw herself onto the bed, and as I pulled off her stockings she pointed her feet like a ballerina. But before I could remove her panties, she pulled the sheet over herself and said, "I'm so tired. The room's spinning around. . . ." Her eyes shut.

I turned out the light and got into bed. Shyly, I put out my hand beneath the sheet and touched the nearer breast. She sighed in her tipsy sleep. "Oh, Rusty . . ." That was chilling. I took the other breast in my hand, and she woke up. "Oh, Myra! You felt just like Rusty." But she pushed my hand away. "He's gentle, too."

"Gentle?" I recalled what Letitia had said. "I thought he was violent!"

"Whatever gave you that idea?" She mumbled, still half asleep. "It's because he was so gentle I loved him. He never grabs you like other boys. . . ."

If nothing else, I have changed at least one young man's sexual performance, and for the good — at least the good of Letitia. From now on Rusty will continue to take out his hatred of me on other women, never realizing to what extent he is really pleasing them. It is ironic what I have inadvertently accomplished. Wanting to tame for all time the archetypal male, I have created something ten times as masculine in the classic sense as what I started with. All in all, not the desired effect but perhaps, like Columbus, I have stumbled on a new world.

I caressed Mary-Ann's breasts, which she allowed . . . but only for a moment; then she turned away from me. "You are an angel, Myra, and I really love you, I do. But I just can't . . . you know . . ."

"Of course I know, dear." And I do; yet I am still profoundly hurt at being rejected.

"If only you were a man or there was a man like you, I'd really fall, I would — but not like this, even with you."

This froze me, turned me to stone.

But why should I care? After all, the silkiness of her body, the tautness of the skin, the firmness of the flesh is neither more nor less appetizing to me than Rusty's body since, in the final analysis (where I am now marooned), a girl is neither more nor less attractive than a boy and I have, God knows, possessed the boy. Yet taking all this into account, there is something about Mary-Ann's wholeness that excites me. There is a mystery to be plumbed, though whether or not it is in her or in myself or in us both I do not know. I did extract a certain pleasure from stroking the body that Rusty had loved, but that victory has already begun to pale. He no longer exists for me. Only the girl he loved matters.

Fortunately, she was compassionate enough to allow me to cradle her in my arms until she fell asleep. Then, when she began softly to snore, obedient to her wishes, I got out of bed and returned to the living room where now I sit at the card table, drinking gin and tonic, writing these lines, too disturbed for sleep.

My head is spinning with fatigue. I must have Mary-Ann but only if she wants me, and that is impossible as things are now. I've just tried to ring Randolph but he gave instructions to the motel operator that he was not to be awakened until morning, the bastard! He knew that I would need to talk to him tonight. Obviously Disneyland was too much for him.

36

Buck's office. I sit at his desk. Randolph sits in the big chair underneath the portrait of Elvis Presley. Buck and his lawyer have gone into the next room to take a telephone call from New York.

As soon as they were out of the room, Randolph wanted to talk but I motioned for him to be quiet. The room is bugged, like everything out here. So Randolph now sits wheezing softly, chewing the stem of his pipe and staring out the window. I write these lines for something to do.

We've shaken them, no doubt of that. But I'm still not certain whether or not they will call our bluff.

Randolph presented them with a signed affidavit, duly notarized, swearing that he had witnessed my wedding to Myron in Monterrey, Mexico. Up until the very last moment I thought I would have trouble with Randolph. Fortunately his greed finally convinced him that he should do the right thing, despite the risk involved. Nevertheless, he is nervous as a cat. So am I.

Buck was true to form. "It was a real nice gesture of your'n, Doc, to come out here and help out this li'l ol' gal." More than ever was Buck, revoltingly, the Singin' Shootin' Cowboy, so inferior in every way to Hoot Gibson. "Naturally we want to do the right thing by her."

"Then cut the cackle," I said firmly, "and hand over the three hundred fifty G's which all of our lawyers now agree is my adjusted share of the property."

"Certainly, Mrs. Breckinridge," said Charlie Flagler Junior. "Just as soon as we get final word, any minute now, from our New York office which will like clear up one final detail, it's all yours because," he turned to Randolph, "we are not about to question the probity of such a well-known person and author like Dr. Montag."

"Thank you," I answered for Randolph, who looked gloomy as he always does when someone praises him (his father withheld all praise during Randolph's formative years and so today he can never accept any compliment without suspecting that it is loaded, as this one of course was).

"Right here," said Buck, holding up a check written on the Bank of America, Beverly Hills Branch, "I've got the check, all made out to you and everything."

Both Randolph and I felt a good deal better at the sight of the loot: three hundred and fifty thousand dollars is more than enough to finance me for the next few years while I finish Myron's work and begin my own. Yes, I have decided to make an investigation in *depth* of the problem of communication in the post-McLuhan world. Each day that I spend in the company of the students makes me more than ever aware that a new world is being born without a single reliable witness except me. I alone have the intuition as well as the profound grasp of philosophy and psychology to trace for man not only what he is but what he must become, once he has ceased to be confined to a single sexual role, to a single person . . . once he has become free to blend with others, to exchange personalities with both men and women, to play out the most elaborate of dreams in a world where there will soon be no limits to the human spirit's play. As I have been goddess, so others can be whatever they want in this vast theatre we call the world where all bodies and all minds will one day be at the disposal of everyone, and no one will read books for that is a solitary activity like going to the bathroom alone (it is the proliferation of private bathrooms, which has, more than anything else, created modern man's sense of alienation from others of his kind: our ancestors bathed and shat together and, all in all, relished the sharing of their common natural functions) or like making love alone if there are others available to share the body's pleasures. I see this new world whose prophetess I am as clearly as I see this page on which I scribble random notes while waiting for Buck and Charlie Flagler Junior to return from their telephoning in the next office.

I have made up my mind to continue teaching here, if Buck will have me . . . which I doubt. Yet I must make the effort to charm him, if it is not too late, for not only am I able to observe and learn from the students but they in turn profit from me. Without the Academy, I would have to invent an equivalent, a place in which to shape the minds of the young, particularly the boys who crave discipline. Yet, oddly enough, since that night of nights in the infirmary all my desires to dominate the male have been — if not satisfied — in abeyance, a true breakthrough, according to Randolph, though he still believes that I went too far and may have damaged Rusty's capacity to love women, to which I responded, "That is exactly what I wanted to do, to teach him fear."

"But why? Why not teach him love?" There are times when Randolph is singularly dense.

"Because only through a traumatic shock, through terrifying and humiliating him, could I hope to change his view of what is proper masculine behavior. To keep him from breeding, and so adding to the world's overpopulation, I was forced to violate everything he has been taught to regard as sacred, including the sanctity of his tiny back door. . . ."

Randolph looked suddenly queasy. "Please, Myra, you know how any *explicit* reference to the anal upsets me. The fault is mine, or weakness I should say," he added quickly, anticipating one of my sharp rejoinders. "But tell me, is there any evidence that your tormenting of him has had any effect at all, good or bad?"

"He quarreled with Mary-Ann . . ."

"A passing fit of ill-temper . . ."

"Not passing. He's left her for Letitia Van Allen." Candid as I always am with Randolph, I have not yet told him the entire story of my maneuvering to keep Rusty and Mary-Ann apart. There is evidence that Rusty is still in love with Mary-Ann. Fortunately she will not, in her present mood, have anything to do with him and I am certain that as long as she is with me I can prolong that mood for quite some time. Also, the fact that Mary-Ann is living with the woman who raped him will unconsciously identify her with me in Rusty's mind; if nothing else, this connection should help to maintain the current distance between the lovers. "And from what Letitia tells me, his lovemaking has been dramatically improved as a result of what I did to him."

"How would you know? He never made love to you."

"Mary-Ann has told me that he was always extremely gentle with her . . . she has a childhood trauma and cannot bear rough lovemaking and so, in time, will be drawn to women who are gentle. But with Letitia, he is a rampaging bull, knocking her about and otherwise getting back at me through her, to her delight of course."

"Interesting" was all that Randolph had to say on the subject. But I can tell that he is impressed at what I have accomplished even though, being a Jew and a dentist, he can never wholeheartedly accept my new order for the human race since the *fluidity* which I demand of the sexes is diametrically opposed to Mosaic solidity. Yet I am right, for it is demonstrably true that desire can take as many shapes as there are containers. Yet what one pours into those containers is always the same inchoate human passion, entirely lacking in definition until what holds it shapes it. So let us break the world's pots, and allow the stuff of desire to flow and intermingle in one great viscous sea. . . .

The door just opened. I keep my head down, continuing to write, pretending to be occupied and not at all eager. From the corner of my eye I can see two human sections approach. One section is brown (Buck) and one is blue (Charlie Flagler Junior). I don't look up. Buck says: "Myron Breckinridge is *not* dead."

BUCK LONER REPORTS —
Recording Disc No. 808 —
1 April

Oh God I dont know if I can stand it
dont know if I can go on its just not worth it re
minder cancel masseuse for rest of week period
paragraph they just left I dont know what to do not
that theres anything I can do caught by the short
hairs by the fickle finger of fate we thought we had
them when this detective in New York came up with
absolute proof that that fag nephew of mine was
not dead because there never was any death certifi
cate issued and New York City is a place where you
cant screw around with that sort of thing unlike
down old Mexico way well Myra who had been sit
ting at my desk pretending to write letters sat up
real smart and said quote I say hes dead and that
means hes dead to which statement Charlie Flagler
Junior replies thinking he has got her over the bar
rel at last not knowing its his turn inside the barrel
quote its not what you say Mrs Breckinridge its

what the police and the city records say and they
say your husband is alive and so his will cant be
probated unquote well she smiled this funny smile
and says quote the body was never found thats true
but he was drowned while cruising the Staten Island
ferry unquote there is says Flagler Junior not one
iota of evidence he is dead so we are not paying you
one single penny until your husband shows up to
collect his share of Mrs Gertrude Percy Breckin
ridges estate unquote then Myra looks at that fat
Jew doctor who is blowing ashes all over my brand
new wall to wall carpeting and she says I quote
Randolph I guess this is the moment of truth un
quote and he nods and allows that maybe shes right
and then so help me god she stands up and hikes up
her dress and pulls down her goddam panties and
shows us this scar where cock and balls should be
and says quote Uncle Buck I am Myron Breckinridge
unquote period paragraph I like to have fainted at
the sight not to mention the news Flagler Junior
just stood there his mouth wide open then Myra or
Myron says quote Randolph can testify to all this
because he was my analyst before the operation
which killed Myron and gave birth to me Myra un
quote the Doc agreed saying I quote I should also
add that I never approved of this operation but My
ron was my friend as well as patient and so when
I saw that there was nothing I could do to talk him
out of this extreme gesture I arranged for the best
surgeon in Copenhagen to perform the operation
two years ago this spring unquote by then Flagler
Junior had got back some of his cool I dont he said
quote believe one word of this story so whoever you
are you may have been a man once but how do
we know that that man was Buck Loners nephew
Myron question mark unquote well that bitch was

ready for that one she opens her handbag with a
smirk and says I quote we had two plans Uncle Buck
one was to get you to accept me as Myrons widow
the other was to prove to you that I used to be Myron
here are Myrons fingerprints from the FBI when he
was fingerprinted as a small boy while visiting the
nations capital with a Boy Scout troop you are free
at any time to check these prints with my own un
quote well thats the ball game I said to Flagler
Junior who still made noises about how did we know
the prints were the same and not just another bluff
so I said I accept the fact that this is my nephew
Myron with his balls cut off like a year old steer
God help us all end quote why Uncle Buck said that
thing quote I am going to kiss you unquote and Buck
Loner who has never been kissed by a man except
by Leo Carrillo in a flick and is all male as the East
West Home Massage Service can almost daily tes
tify allowed himself to be kissed by that goddam
thing that creep that capon oh screams Myron after
he has got his goddam lipstick all over my ear I
knew wed be great friends one day ever since I used
to see every single picture you ever made and wrote
you all those fan letters yes I said I sure remember
those letters and I told Gertrude that you were ob
viously bright as they come so now Myron no no no
it says to me Im Myra Myron is dead as a doornail
why when I lost those ugly things it was like a ship
losing its anchor and Ive been sailing ever since
havent I Randolph free as a bird and perfectly happy
in being the most extraordinary woman in the world
unquote well what can you say to that question
mark I said nothing but just handed her the check
which she put in her handbag Ill cash it this after
noon he she said oh he she was bright as can be all
smiles now that the moolah has been handed over

but then on top of that she delivers the whammy
quote you know Uncle Buck we make a wonderful
team together you and I and so I thought if you
didnt mind that Id just keep on teaching here for
the rest of the year after all youve got to admit that
Ive done well and now that Letitia Van Allen is my
best girl friend I can help the students achieve real
stardom end quote well I tried to be as polite as pos
sible under the circumstances and so I said quote
Myron Myra I said thats not true only with these two
me your services here and theres no doubt about it
but that youre a crackerjack teacher a little strict
maybe and sometimes maybe a mite too sharp in
what you say but all in all youve been a real asset
to the Academy as I am the first to admit only thing
is weve got two former teachers returning who have
like tenure and one wants to take over Posture and
the other Empathy well she was not about to be
conned I quote apparently what youre trying to say
Myra said in this awful low voice she sometimes
uses that now I recognize is a mans voice quote is
that you dont want me here at all end quote now
Myron Myra I said thats not true only with these two
coming back but I was interrupted again when My
ron came up to me and grabbed me by the collar
that little bastard is strong as they come ball less
or not listen Buck he says tough as nails quote if
you dont give me a job I am going to announce to
the world that Buck Loners nephew became his
niece two years ago in Copenhagen and that will fix
your wagon in this town unquote thats blackmail
said Flagler Junior but nobody paid him any mind
OK Myra I said you win end quote then she was all
smiles again I knew youd do the right thing Uncle
Buck and I can help you I really can Jesus God what
am I going to do now with this mad freak taking

over my life and running the Academy that I built
up on dreams and hopes which she believes in de
stroying by telling everybody whats wrong with him
if I could get away with it I would kill her strike
that period paragraph

37

Tomorrow is moving day. I have rented a house just above Santa Monica Canyon. A superb view of the Pacific Palisades somewhat compensates for the inevitable view of that despicable body of water, drowning the horizon to the west and all Asia.

So now I sit for the last time looking out upon the giant turning woman who holds her sombrero like a benediction over those who pass beneath her on the Strip.

I am not at all certain what to do about Mary-Ann. I know that I want her to live with me always. I know that I want to possess her entirely, body as well as mind; yet I puzzle myself, and Randolph has been no help at all. He has, incidentally, decided to stay on for one more week but of course that one week will become a lifetime. He is made for Hollywood and Hollywood is made for him, particularly now that he has discovered the Will Wright Ice Cream Parlors.

This morning Randolph again challenged my theory of sex. He maintains that the desire to possess another person's body simply as a means of achieving power is only one part of an infinitely complex response. To a point, I agree with him. It is certainly true that, power aside, a certain amount of tenderness is necessary in human relations. Myron never understood this and it is possible that no man really can. Yet we women are instinctively tender, even when we are achieving total dominion. As a woman, I was touched by Rusty's tears. I even experienced a maternal warmth while tidying up his poor bloody bottom. That is woman's role, to make the wound and then to heal it. Not for nothing do the earliest of myths depict us as Fate itself, attending the male from swaddling clothes to winding sheet. But there has been nothing in my experience which has quite prepared me for Mary-Ann. Of course she is unique in her charm, her beauty, her womanliness. I have never known a girl who could arouse in me so many conflicting emotions. Even the uterine mysteries, so deplored by Myron, are now for me the be-all and end-all, the center to which one must return and not simply in search of Rusty's phallic track but for the sake of the journey itself to the very source of life.

We had dinner tonight with Letitia at Scandia, an excellent restaurant on the Strip where Scandinavian food is served to a most elegant clientele, among whom I counted four bona fide stars of the Forties.

It took me an entire day to talk Mary-Ann into having dinner with Letitia, whom she regards as "the other woman." She only agreed when I assured her that Letitia was the one being used by Rusty, not the other way around. Letitia and I had agreed on this approach when I saw her briefly this afternoon at the office. The poor woman's arm was in a sling but otherwise she was in splendid form. "*He* sprained it last night!" she exclaimed fondly. "I thought he was going to break every bone in my body!"

"And you really enjoy that?" It seemed to me incredible that a fellow goddess could endure such treatment from a mere man.

"I never knew what sex was until that little bastard moved in. Four, five times a night on the floor, on the beach, in the damned bathtub!" She looked misty at the recollection. My own experience of that small limp rose was obviously not the entire truth.

Then Letitia congratulated me on my appointment as co-director of the Academy. The announcement appeared in all the trade papers last Monday and so I am now, to my amusement, a figure in the world of show biz — which of course has only the most shadowy of connections with the world of mythic films.

"Yes, Uncle Buck and I seem to be getting on better." Buck has, in fact, completely surrendered and for the past week I have been running the Academy. As a result, morale is infinitely higher at every level. Even Dark Laughter found creative some of my suggestions for including Dionysian elements in his Atavistic Rhythm classes. Morning, noon and night I am Rosalind Russell, efficient girl executive, and the students are the better for my constant brisk encouragement.

I came to the point. "As you know, Mary-Ann is living with me. Now don't smile like that, nothing dikey has happened or will. But I do feel responsible for the poor kid. And that's why I'd like to know just what Rusty is going to do about her."

"Not a damned thing if I can help it." Letitia was hard as nails. "I'm hanging onto that stud for as long as I can."

"That suits me. But what about him?"

"Mr. Martinson!" Letitia gave a laugh which started out to be tinkling but quickly became not unlike the minatory rattle of a leper's bell. I should have known that Letitia would be as clever as I. She too, has Rusty by the balls. "We're on good terms, Mr. Martinson and I, and he thinks if anybody can make something of the boy it will be me."

"So if Rusty decides to stray . . ."

"Mr. Martinson will bring him back." Letitia sighed contentedly. Then she frowned. "But there's no doubt about it, he's still interested in Mary-Ann, even though he can't get over the fact that she's living with you. He absolutely hates you, darling. Why? He won't tell me."

"And never will." I daresay I looked as pleased as I felt. "Anyway, that's all in the past. Now I want you to have dinner with Mary-Ann and me and I want you to convince her that Rusty was just using you and that now he's off with someone else."

Letitia wondered if this was a wise tactic. I assured her that it was, and I was right. Our dinner at Scandia was a success. Mary-Ann got tiddly on snaps and, all in all, we were like three schoolgirls on the town. Mary-Ann soon forgave Letitia. "I understand what you must've felt. I mean, he's the most wonderful boy there is and I don't suppose any woman could resist him."

"I tried," said Letitia solemnly, stroking her sprained arm in its sling. "God knows I tried."

"I guess it was too much for me to hope to keep him." Mary-Ann was close to tears but we both did our best to cheer her up, assuring her of future boyfriends not to mention the prospect of stardom which Letitia dangled before our eyes, a dream made all the more palpable by the sudden appearance of a major television personality who embraced Letitia and complained, "You never call me!" Mary-Ann and I were duly impressed by this public display of Letitia's greatness, and flattered that we are now her friends.

After saying good night to Letitia, Mary-Ann and I came back to the apartment. We are both a little sad at the thought of leaving our first home together. But we are also excited at the thought of the new house, particularly the soundproofed music room where Mary-Ann will practice. She has become, suddenly, grimly ambitious. She means to be a major star and if she does not attain at least the magnitude of Susanna Foster my name is not Myra Breckinridge. In fact, according to Miss Cluff, there is a thrilling new quality to Mary-Ann's voice which "I'm sure staying with you and receiving a *woman's* love and guidance has given her." Miss Cluff giggled despite my coldness, for I do not want her — or anybody — to think that either of us is one of *les girls*. I must protect Mary-Ann. I must also protect myself since I can never rule out the possibility that some day I shall find that perfect man who will totally resist me and so win my love, and hand in marriage.

I find that lately I've been prone to the most sickening sentimental reveries, usually involving Mary-Ann though sometimes a faceless man is at my side and we live together in an enchanted cottage filled with the pitter-pat of little feet or I should say paws since I detest children but have lately come to adore dogs. First thing Monday, Mary-Ann and I are going to the kennel and buy two wirehaired terriers, "Hers" and "Hers" — in memory of Asta, that sweet dog who was in the *Thin Man* series with William Powell and Myrna Loy.

Tonight our love took on a new dimension. Mary-Ann now undresses in front of me. She then lies on the bed, eyes tight shut, lovely breasts fallen back upon themselves; and as I trace their contours with a finger, causing them to tighten visibly, she sighs with pleasure which is the signal for me to begin with my hand the exploration of that pale dimpled belly which curves its secret way to the blonde silky thatch so often penetrated by Rusty but still forbidden to me. In fact, every time my hand approaches that secret and for me so beautifully enticing and *central* reality, the cave of origin, she turns away and whispers, "No."

But tonight she was subtly changed. I don't know whether it was the snaps at Scandia or the cold bright charm of the powerful Letitia or the knowledge that Rusty would never be hers again but whatever it was, she allowed my hand to rest a long moment on the entrance to the last fantasy which is of course the first reality. Ecstatically, I fingered the lovely shape whose secret I must know or die, whose maze I must thread as best I can or go mad for if I am to prevail I must soon come face to face with the Minotaur of dreams and confound him in his charneled lair, and in our heroic coupling know the last mystery: total power achieved not over man, not over woman but over the heraldic beast, the devouring monster, the maw of creation itself that spews us forth and sucks us back into the black oblivion where stars are made and energy waits to be born in order to begin once more the cycle of destruction and creation at whose apex now I stand, once man, now woman, and soon to be privy to what lies beyond the uterine door, the mystery of creation that I mean to shatter with the fierce thrust of a will that alone separates me from the nothing of eternity; and as I have conquered the male, absorbed and been absorbed by the female, I am at last outside the human scale, and so may render impotent even familiar banal ubiquitous death whose mouth I see smiling at me with moist coral lips between the legs of my beloved girl who is the unwitting instrument of victory, and the beautiful fact of my life's vision made all too perfect flesh.

When at last she pulled away from me, she seemed almost reluctant, as though she wanted me to continue and achieve for her that orgasm which tonight I could sense was near. "Myra, don't. It spoils it."

"Darling, whatever you want." I have learned restraint, unlike Myron who could not be deterred from the object of his lust by even a teeth-rattling fist in his poor face. But Myron was tortured by having been attached to those male genitals which are linked to a power outside the man who sports them or, to be precise, they

sport the man for they are peculiarly willful and separate
and it is not for nothing that the simple boy so often says
of his erection, partly as a joke but partly as a frightening
fact, "He's got a head of his own." Indeed *he* has a head
of his own and twice I have punished that head. Once by
a literal decapitation, killing Myron so that Myra might
be born and then, symbolically, by torturing and mock-
ing Rusty's sex in order to avenge Myron for the count-
less times that he had been made victim by that mitred
one-eyed beast, forever battering blindly at any orifice,
seeking to scatter wide the dreaded seed that has already
so filled up the world with superfluous people that our
end is now at hand: through war and famine and the
physical decadence of a race whose extinction is not only
inevitable but, to my mind, desirable . . . for after me
what new turn can the human take? Once I have com-
prehended the last mystery I shall be free to go without
protest, full of wisdom, into night, happy in the knowledge that, above all men, I existed totally. Let the dust
take me when the adventure's done and I shall make that
dust glitter for all eternity with my marvelous fury.
Meanwhile, I must change the last generation of man. I
must bring back Eden. And I can, I am certain, for if
there is a god in the human scale, I am she.

And so, unlike Myron, I am able to be loving and gentle. I am able to hold Mary-Ann in my arms as a mother
cradles a child or as I hold a fox terrier puppy who has
taken my fancy.

"I love being with you — like this," she said tonight,
eyes shut, smiling.

"I love it, too." I was simple. "It's all I want, making

you happy." I squeezed her bare shoulders; our breasts touched, teasingly. Mine are even larger than hers, filled with silicone, the result of a new process discovered in France and not always successful in its application (recently a French stripper died when the silicone was injected by mistake into an artery). I was fortunate, however, and no one, not even a trained physician, can tell that my beautiful firm breasts are not the real thing.

Shyly, Mary-Ann once said, "They're just super, Myra! I bet the boys were really after you in high school." An amusing thought since, in those days, it was I who was after the boys. At fourteen Myron vowed that he would, in one way or another, extract the essence of every good-looking boy in school and he succeeded in one hundred and one cases over a three-year period, a time in his life which he used to refer to as the Scheherazade phase, the hundred and one nights — or possibly "flights" is the better word to describe what he did with those birdlike objects whose thrust so fascinated him but so disgusts me, for I have got past that crude *obvious* instrument of procreation to the deep center where all is veiled, and purest magic.

But Mary-Ann is making progress; her admiration of my body is not entirely aesthetic . . . but then the body in question is, if I may say so, unusually lovely, the result of the most dedicated of plastic surgeons who allowed me, at my request, to remain conscious during all stages of my transformation, even though I was warned that I might be seriously traumatized in the process.

But I was not. Quite the contrary. I was enthralled, delighted, fascinated (of course the anesthetic had a somewhat intoxicating effect). And when, with one swift movement of the scalpel, the surgeon freed me from the detested penis, I amazed everyone by beginning to sing, I don't know why, "I'll be seeing you" . . . hardly a fitting song since the point to the exercise is that I would *not* be seeing it or any of its equivalents, except for that of the tortured Rusty, ever again; at least not in the way Myron saw such things.

Nevertheless, I was elated, and have not for one moment regretted my decision to be unique. That my plans have lately gone somewhat awry is the sort of risk one must take if life is to be superb. For instance, I had always believed that between the operation, on the one hand, and the rape of someone like Rusty on the other, I would become Woman Triumphant, exercising total power over men as men once exerted that same power over Myron and still do over the usual woman. But the very literalness of my victory deprived me of the anticipated glory. To my astonishment, I have now lost all interest in men. I have simply gone past them, as if I were a new creation, a mutant diverging from original stock to become something quite unlike its former self or any self known to the race. All that I want now in the way of human power is to make Mary-Ann love me so that I might continue to love her — even without possessing her — to the end of my days.

Imagine my consternation when, once again, she said what she truly felt (and what I have known all along but refused to let myself admit even to myself): "If you were only a man, Myra, I would love you so!"

Of course the shock of the anticipated is always more

intense than that of the unexpected. I let her go, as though her cool body had turned suddenly to flame. "Love is not always a matter of sex," I said weakly.

"Oh, I know. And I do love you, as you are. I even like it when you touch me, up to a point," she added judiciously, "but it's really only with a boy I can let myself go. That's the way I am."

"Rusty?"

She shut her eyes, frowning with recollected pain. "No. That's finished. But someone like him." She sighed, "And there aren't many."

"Not many!" I was tactless, and harsh. "The garages of America are crowded with Rustys."

She shook her head. "No. He *is* special. Most boys grab. He doesn't. He's so sweet in bed, and that's what I like. I can't stand the other. I never could. That first boy almost turned me off for good, in high school. He was like a maniac, all over me!" She shuddered at the memory. "In a funny way," she said, "you remind me of Rusty, the way you touch me."

As I write these lines at the card table, facing the Château Marmont and the solemnly turning chorine, I feel the tears rising. What am I to do?

Randolph has been useless. This morning I met him at Will Wright's on the Strip, near Larue's. He was already halfway through a double chocolate burnt-almond and pistachio sundae, gaining the sort of oral gratification that, were he not a puritan Jew, a cock might have provided, with far fewer calories. But he is hopeless. His first and only marriage ended after one year and though he has not confided in me what went wrong, I suspect that he was inadequate if not impotent. Since then, as far as I know, only the theory of sex interests him; the real thing causes him a profound distress which he relieves with food.

"You must tell her everything, if you love her," was his profound advice, as he munched on three maraschino cherries.

"I can't."

"Why not? You wish to exert power over her . . ."

"Only that she may exert it over me . . ."

"So power is intransitive as well as transitive? Then you are clearly moving into a new phase."

"Whatever the phase, I don't know what to do. If I tell her that I used to be Myron, I destroy Myra . . ."

"Not a bad idea."

I was furious. "You always preferred Myron to me, didn't you?" I let him have it. "And I know why. You were in love with him, you God-damned closet-queen!"

But in my fury I had misplayed my hand for this is exactly the sort of scene Randolph delights in. Carefully he put down his spoon, licked his chops and said, "That's very interesting, what you say. Now tell me exactly: why do you feel that friendship must invariably have an *overt* sexual connotation when your own experience . . ."

"Darling Randolph, why don't you go fuck yourself? It would be an act of some mercy, and therapeutic, too."

There is nothing more satisfactory than to be at last entirely free of one's analyst, and I am rid of mine. The end occurred when I found myself deeply resenting having to pay him forty-two thousand five hundred dollars for perjuring himself when, as things turned out, I didn't need his help at all.

Unfortunately, Randolph chooses to interpret my harsh dismissal as a new symptom of neurosis. "We're making splendid progress," he exclaimed, pig's eyes gleaming with excitement. "Now let's go back a moment. The emotional trigger, as usual, is your fear that I preferred Myron to you . . ."

"Look, I couldn't care less who or what you prefer. Your feelings are your own problem. My only concern in this world is not you and your gluttony (a sex life must be ruled out), but Mary-Ann . . ."

"Wonderful! This is the big breakthrough we've been waiting for! By saying that I have no sex life . . ."

". . . is apt to leave me if she knows that I used to be a man . . ."

". . . you must be able to visualize . . ."

". . . and I couldn't bear that. Yet if I don't tell her . . ."

". . . me having sexual relations with Myron. Now then, how exactly do you see me in the act? Active or passive . . ."

". . . I'll lose her to the first light-fingered stud who comes her way . . ."

". . . would I be oral in my desires or anal or . . ."

"From the way you eat, oral! Randolph, you disgust me, you really do!" Like all analysts, Randolph is interested only in himself. In fact, I have often thought that the analyst should pay the patient for allowing himself to be used as a captive looking-glass. "I take it all back," I said curtly. "I didn't mean a word of it."

"*Consciously* this may be true, but to have made the accusation you did reveals . . ."

I left him and crossed the street to where my car was parked, nearly getting myself run over by one of those maniac drivers who make walking so perilous in the Greater Los Angeles area. But then the pedestrian is not favored hereabouts. In fact, the police are quick to stop and question anyone found on foot in a residential district since it is a part of California folklore that only the queer or criminal walk; the good drive cars that fill the air with the foul odor of burning fossils, and so day by day our lungs fill up with the stuff of great ferns and dinosaurs who thus revenge themselves upon their successors, causing us to wither and die prematurely.

As I watch the Las Vegas chorine turn and turn, I find myself thinking, not unnaturally, of *Turnabout* (1937), with Adolphe Menjou, Carole Landis and adorable John Hubbard; and I ponder that brilliant plot in which husband and wife exchange personalities through the magic of the talking film (he speaks with her voice, she with his) and, as Parker Tyler puts it so well, we have, as a result, "a realization of ancient magical belief in the guise of modern make-believe, and the same ambiguity and ambivalence of spiritual essences are revealed that modern psychology, especially psychoanalysis, has uncovered in present-day civilization."

My worn copy of Tyler's *Magic and Myth of the Movies* is always open before me when I write, and I constantly search the familiar text for guidance. But tonight I can find nothing more comforting than Tyler's suggestion (referring to *Turnabout* and the Warsaw Art

Players' film *The Dybbuk*, which also deals with the idea of possession) "that by *imitating* the female the male believes that he *becomes* the female, thus automatically and unconsciously practicing the imitative variety of sympathetic magic." Of course magic was involved at the beginning of my quest. But I have since crossed the shadow line, made magic real, created myself. But to what end? For what true purpose have I smashed the male principle only to become entrapped by the female? Something must soon be done or I am no longer triumphant, no longer the all-conquering Myra Breckinridge . . . whisper her name! Sympathetic magic must be made. But how?

38

I must record my situation exactly. They say that I am under sedation. That means I have been drugged. They are holding me against my will. But I shall outwit them.

The one who calls himself Dr. Mengers has already fallen into my trap. When I asked for this notebook, he granted my wish. "Excellent therapy," he said, assuming a bedside manner that even a child could detect was false. He is with the CIA. They all are. He pretended to take my pulse. "Much better today. Very much better. It was touch and go for a while, you know. But you've pulled through with flying colors!"

I played my part with magnificent cunning. I fell in with the game, pretended that I had been ill, made my voice even weaker than it is. "Tell me, Doctor," I quavered, "how long have I been here, like this?"

"Ten days. Out cold," he said with all-too-obvious satisfaction.

For ten days they have held me captive! But now for

reasons of their own, they are bringing me around, and that is their mistake for when it comes to a contest of wills, I am bound to win, even in my present hallucinated condition.

"When can I get up?" I whispered.

"Not for a week at least. As you see, you are in a plaster cast from neck to ankles. But your arms are free." He pinched me hard above the elbow. "Does that hurt?"

He is a sadist, too. I refused to give him the satisfaction of crying out. "Certainly not," I said, and he frowned and made a note in a little black code book. Obviously I am a tougher nut to crack than he thought. Yet what I fear is not torture but the various drugs and serums that they have obviously been giving me from the look of my arms, which are blue, black and yellow with bruises and punctures. Not even a woman as brave and unique as I can hope to withstand an all-out chemical assault upon the brain and nervous system.

What have I told them? Did I reveal the secret of human destiny to the enemy? I pray not. But only a careful questioning of my captors will be able to set my mind at rest. If I *have* told all, then there is no hope for the coming breakthrough. They will do to me what they did to Mossadegh in Iran and Arbenz in Guatemala.

We were then joined by the "nurse." Even for the CIA she was a poor actress, obviously recruited at the last minute, assuming that she is not the mistress of some Pentagon bureaucrat. She approached me with a thermometer as though she were uncertain as to how to go about placing the object in question in my mouth. She was plainly nervous and ill at ease. But then the ther-

mometer was drugged and it is possible that she was experiencing a momentary twinge of conscience, quickly
dispelled by the "doctor," who had been watching her
with ill-disguised irritation.

"Go on, take the temperature. Please," he said in an
irritable voice.

"But he bit my finger last time," she said plaintively, as
I allowed the thermometer to be placed beneath my
tongue.

"But Mr. Breckinridge was delirious at the time. Now
he's quite normal."

"What do you mean *Mr*. Breckinridge?" I asked, suddenly aware of the shift in sex, and nearly swallowing the
thermometer in the process. They exchanged a conspiratorial look, much like the one Oswald gave Ruby on television seconds before he was struck down by his supposed friend and accomplice.

"Of course, *Miss* Breckinridge," said the "doctor"
soothingly, readjusting the thermometer. I made no further complaint although I prefer the honorific title of
Mrs., to which my uniqueness entitles me.

"I still have an ugly scar," said the "nurse," holding up
a bandaged hand in an effort to engage the "doctor's"
sympathy. I was pleased with myself: apparently I had
fought hard to retain my mind's integrity so rudely violated by these drug-administering agents of imperialism.

"Now, Nurse, we must try and understand what he
. . . what she has had to go through these last few
days."

"What *we've* had to go through," grumbled the

"nurse," at the very least the mistress of an Assistant Secretary of Defense, so cheeky is she.

Her superior was coldly unsympathetic (obviously a division in their ranks; one I shall exploit). "I suggest we tend to our job, Nurse, and take the rough with the smooth."

"Yes, Doctor." She tried to sound chastened but failed. Then she withdrew the theromometer and said, "Normal," and looked disappointed. It is quite evident that they want me to die of what appear to be natural causes. Fortunately, my body will no more surrender to their poison than my mind has. I shall outwit them all, and prevail! If they mean to kill me they will have to take direct action, and so leave clues.

"Good news!" The charlatan beamed, writing in his code book. "We've passed the danger mark and I'm pleased as all get-out!"

Get out, I thought, smiling bravely, like . . . what's her name in . . . my memory seems to have left me. The drugs must have been enormously powerful. Or did they use electroshock treatments? That would explain my condition like who was it in . . . I can't recall that film's title either. Whole sections of memory are missing. But I shall regain them: it is simply a matter of will. Meanwhile, they are certain that I can find no way of getting a message to the outside world but in this, as in everything, they underestimate me.

They are gone now. I am sitting up in a metal bed placed at the center of a small cell disguised as a hospital room. There is even the awful odor of disinfectant to lend verisimilitude to the otherwise ridiculous decor. Any fool can see that this is a prison, not a hospital. Why else are the venetian blinds shut?

I am encased in what appears to be plaster of Paris from neck to ankle. Inside this carapace I can hardly move. My legs feel as if they had just been asleep and now, tingling, are coming to life again. I can wiggle my feet: that is something, and my poor arms, though discolored, are intact and I suppose, in time, I shall be able to peel off this plaster strait jacket . . . unless of course they keep such careful watch over me that any attempt at freeing myself will be thwarted. At the moment, it is my intelligence upon which I must rely.

I cannot recall the name of Lana Turner's first film! Something *has* been done to my brain. I know that I am Myra Breckinridge whom no man may possess, but what else? Film titles are lost to me. The past is a jumble. I must not panic.

What's the last thing I can recall before they captured me? This is difficult. Santa Monica. The mesa? No. Not mesa. A word like it. Canyon. The Santa Monica Canyon. A winding road. Sun in my eyes as I drive. Alone? Yes, alone. No one is in the car. A dog? Yes, a wirehaired fox terrier puppy. Sitting on my lap. Sun in my eyes. That means it was late afternoon and I am coming *from* Hollywood to the sea — oh, the mind of Myra Breckinridge can never be broken or too long deranged, even by the CIA!

I park the car in front of a small house, green with white shutters, overlooking the ugly ocean. Fortress? Canal? Pilings? Palisades . . . that's it: Pacific Palisades are visible. It's our house. Ours? Who else? No. I'm going too fast now and my head is throbbing. Sodium pentothal obviously.

I park the car on the main road. I get out of the car. I stand and wait for the dog to jump out. The dog does. He runs up the driveway. He stops at the door of the house. I start to follow then

39

Struck by a hit-and-run automobile, I have been unconscious for ten days. I sustained twelve broken ribs, one cracked femur, one fractured shin, a dozen torn and bruised ligaments, as well as a concussion of the brain. Only my powerful *physical* organism was able to save me, according to Dr. Mengers, who has been an absolute saint during my ordeal.

"Frankly we didn't think you were going to make it," he said earlier this evening. "But the first moment I saw you I said to myself: that one's going to put up a good fight, and you did. The night nurse is still home, convalescing."

"Night nurse? What did I do?"

"Bit her arm to the bone."

We had a merry laugh about that. Then I spoke seriously. "I'm worried about my memory, Doctor. For instance, I can recall the stars of *The Uninvited* (Ray Milland, Ruth Hussey, Donald Crisp) and I know that

Charles Brackett produced the film for Paramount in 1944 but who . . . *who* was the director?"

"Lewis Allen." He did not pause to think.

I was momentarily distracted from my own problems at finding a doctor who knew so much about movies. Apparently he too had seen every film made between 1931 and 1947. He was even, for a short time, Roland Young's physician. We exchanged movie lore excitedly, and as we did, I found myself recalling more and more details which I had thought were forever lost to me. But not until I listed every film Edith Head had worked on did Dr. Mengers show his delight. "You see? You *can* remember. It's just a matter of practice. Nothing serious has happened to your mind. With the sort of concussion you sustained, it is like having the wind knocked out of you . . . takes time to catch your breath. Don't worry. You're doing fine."

I was relieved, to say the least. I have every confidence in this marvelous doctor who is to me now more friend than physician. So close do I feel to him that I am able to confide in him. I did this evening, though not without a degree of embarrassment.

"Dr. Mengers, I realize I'm not looking my best, what with this turban which is not exactly flattering to my delicate features, and being all bruised, but there is one thing that does alarm me. I seem to be . . ." I could hardly get the words out. "I seem to be growing a beard."

He became immediately evasive. Why? In the vaguest of terms, he told me not to worry; he even suggested that I *shave!* To which I responded, rather sharply, that a woman who takes a razor to her face may as well say farewell to her femininity. "What I plainly need," I said, coming to the point, "is a massive shot of female hormones."

"I'm afraid that's out of the question in your present condition. Such an injection would interfere seriously with the healing process. Later, perhaps." But though he was soothing, I detect something very odd in his manner. Is it possible that my first impression was correct? That there is indeed a plot against me? I must be on my guard at all times and not allow myself to be lulled into a sense of false security by a man who *claims* to be a doctor but knows altogether too much about films.

Apparently Mary-Ann has been trying to see me. She comes to the hospital every day, the adorable girl! I told Dr. Mengers to tell her that I love her dearly and when I am looking less ghastly I will see her. Meanwhile, I talk to her twice a day on the telephone.

"You don't know what I've been through!" she exclaimed when she first heard my voice, and promptly burst into tears of joy. I'm afraid I wept, too, at the sound of my darling's voice. In any case, all is well at the house. The dogs are almost housebroken though there are still occasional accidents, particularly on the new curtains in the living room. Mary-Ann continues her singing lessons and attends the Academy where I am much missed. Buck inquires daily about my health and Dr. Montag is coming to see me tomorrow.

The driver of the car that struck me has not yet been apprehended. The police hope for me to give them some clue but I cannot. I have no memory of anything once the dog ran up the garden walk. Apparently I was struck from behind.

Was it an accident, or was it . . . who? Rusty? Buck? I am suddenly filled with suspicion. Two weeks ago I was almost run over in front of Larue's. A coincidence? Well, if either of those sons-of-bitches did this to me I will have his God-damned head or my name is not Myron Breckinridge!

40

The room is filled with the smell of Randolph's pipe. Across the floor, burnt-out cinders indicate his various maneuvers. He was in good form. So am I, despite constant headaches and the odd sensation that my legs are filled with burning pins. Fortunately the cast will be removed tomorrow.

To my surprise, Randolph did not think me paranoid when I told him my suspicions.

"It crossed my mind, too," he said, sucking at his pipe. "It could very well have been Rusty's revenge."

"Or Buck Loner's. He would do anything to remove me from the Academy. Even murder."

Yet as I gave voice to my suspicions I cannot, in my heart of hearts, really believe that anyone in his right mind could wish to remove me from a world so desperately in need of me. I prefer to have faith in my fellowman. I must even have a certain tenderness for him if I am to change, through example as well as teaching, his attitude toward sex. There was a time in our evolution when hate alone was motor to our deeds. But that age is ending, for I mean to bring to the world love of the sort that I have learned from Mary-Ann, a love which, despite its intensity, is mere prelude to something else again, to a new dimension which I alone am able to perceive, if dimly. Once I have formulated it, the true mission will begin. But for now I must be cryptic and declare that nothing is what it seems and what nothing seems is false.

"I would suspect Rusty more than Buck," said Randolph, plunging his thick paws into the huge get-well basket of fruit sent me "with love" from Uncle Buck and Bobbie Dean Loner. Randolph crushed a peach against his jaws. I looked away. "The motive in the case of Rusty is more profound psychologically." Randolph's teeth struck the peach's pit with a grating sound that sent shivers along my spine.

"Well, it's done and past. And I'm willing to forgive whoever it was."

"Are you really?" Randolph sounded surprised, not prepared for the new me.

"Of course. Suffering ennobles, doesn't it?" I had no desire to confide in Randolph, particularly now when I am assembling an entirely new personality with which to take the world by storm. "But I do wish you'd talk to Dr. Mengers and ask him to give me a hormone cocktail. I'm sprouting hair in all directions."

Randolph wiped his lips free of peach juice with a banana which he then unpeeled. "Yes, he told me about your request. Unfortunately, it's medically dangerous at the moment."

"But I can't let Mary-Ann see me like this."

"I'm sure she'll understand."

Before I could remonstrate with Randolph, he was launched upon one of his monologues whose subject, as usual, was Randolph Spenser Montag.

". . . office in Brentwood, a quiet neighborhood. Many of my patients live nearby which makes things easy for them if not for me. I've already made the down payment on the house, which is Spanish-style ranch-type, and so I should be ready for business in a few weeks. Culturally the Los Angeles area is far richer than I had dreamed, with many extremely stimulating people . . ."

I was spared Randolph's rationalizations by the sudden opening of the door and the nurse shouting, "Surprise, surprise!"

The surprise was an incline board on wheels which the nurse rolled backwards into the room, to my amazement. Was I expected to get on it and be wheeled about like a sacred relic or Pharaonic mummy? The mystery was solved when, with a flourish, the nurse spun the thing around to reveal Letitia Van Allen in a neck brace, strapped to the board.

"Darling!" Letitia was exuberant, despite the strangeness of her position. "Thank God, you're conscious! We were so worried!"

"I'm Dr. Montag," said Randolph gravely, never one to be kept for long out of a conversation. I made the introductions.

"Sorry I can't shake hands." Letitia was intrepid. "My

neck is fractured and two spinal discs have fused. Otherwise I'm in a great shape."

The nurse agreed. Obviously she worships Letitia. "Miss Van Allen is just *bursting* with energy. It's all we could do to keep her in traction."

"How long have you been here?" I asked, suspecting what had happened.

"Two days after your accident, I took a header on the stairs at Malibu, and here I am, getting the first real rest I've had in twenty years."

"Except she's a naughty girl and not resting at all." The nurse was adoring. "She has moved her whole office into the hospital. You should see her room. It's a madhouse!"

"Sweetie, will you mix us a nice martini? Beefeater gin, no vermouth, on the rocks, with just the tiniest dash of rock salt."

"Oh, Miss Van Allen, you know hospital rules . . ."

"And a glass of champagne for yourself. Hurry up now! Letitia is parched."

The nurse departed. Letitia beamed at us. Then she frowned. "Angel, what's wrong with your face? It looks like you're . . ."

". . . growing a beard." I sighed. "Well, I am. A result of some sort of hormonal imbalance caused by the accident. Isn't that right, Doctor?"

Randolph blew sparks at Letitia, and agreed, at convincing quasi-scientific length. All the while, Letitia was studying me with a thoughtful look. I cursed myself for not having used a thick foundation makeup.

"You know," said Letitia, when Randolph had wheezed into silence, "you would make a marvelous-looking man. Really, Myra, I mean it."

"Don't be silly!" I grew hot with anxiety, as well as rage at Dr. Mengers for not having done more to prevent this dreadful, if temporary, reversion to my original state.

"Darling, I didn't mean it as an insult! Quite the contrary. In fact . . ." Letitia apologized at length as we drank the martinis the nurse brought us and watched Randolph break open a large pineapple and tear at its tallowy flesh.

After what seemed an age of small talk, Randolph finished the pineapple and, with many a puff and wheeze and groan, got to his feet and said good-by.

The moment the door shut behind him, Letitia flew across the room on her incline board, coming to a full stop beside my bed. "It was perfection!" She roared happily. "Total perfection! I have never in my life known such total and complete happiness. Such a . . . no, there are no words to describe what I went through. All I know is that I am now *entirely* fulfilled. I have lived and I have loved to the fullest! I can at last give up sex because anything more would be anticlimax."

"Not to mention fatal." I must say Letitia's happiness depressed me mortally. "Just what did Rusty do to you this time?"

"What did he *not* do!" Her eyes became glazed with memory and gin. "It all happened the day he signed the contract at Fox. You know I got him the lead in that series with top money, special billing, participation, the works. Anyway, after the signing, we went back to Malibu to celebrate." Her voice was dreamy. "It began upstairs when he tore my clothes off in the closet. Then he raped me standing up with a metal clothes hanger twisted around my neck, choking me. I could hardly breathe. It was exquisite! Then one thing led to another. Those small attentions a girl like me cherishes . . . a lighted cigarette stubbed out on my derriere, a complete beating with his great thick heavy leather belt, a series of ravenous bites up and down the inner thighs, drawing blood. All the usual fun things, except that this time he went beyond anything he had ever tried before. This time he dragged me to the head of the stairs and raped me from behind, all the while beating me with his boot. Then, just as I was about to reach the big O, shrieking with pleasure, he hurled me down the stairs, so that my orgasm and the final crash with the banister occurred simultaneously. I fainted with joy! Without a doubt, it was the completion of my life."

"And here you are, half paralyzed." I could not resist being sour.

"Only temporarily. But I agree, one more go and I'll be dead, which is why we've agreed not to see each other again, except in a business way."

"He no longer needs you, so he drops you."

"You are a case, Myra!" Letitia tolled a great bronze laugh. "Actually the opposite is true. Since he's going to be a star he'll need me more than ever, in the business way. No, these things run their course. Frankly I don't think I shall ever again need sex. Once you have known the kind of perfection that I obtained at the moment of collision with that banister, anything else is too second-rate to be endured. I am a fulfilled woman, perhaps the only one in the world."

I must say I can only admire (and perhaps envy) Letitia. Not since the early Betty Hutton films has female masochism been so beautifully served. But I have my own problems. I come straight to the point. "Will Rusty go back to Mary-Ann?"

"Never. He's playing the field now. He's taking a bachelor pad with that young stud who was just let go by Universal — John Edward Jane."

"So you think he'll settle down to a life of promiscuity." I was relieved.

"After me, where can he go? Don't worry. He's lost all interest in your girlfriend."

This was said gaily. Even so, I felt shame, not so much for myself as for Mary-Ann.

"She's *not* my girlfriend. She has a horror of Lesbianism."

"That you don't share. Oh, come off it, Myra. You can tell your pal Letitia. Why, we've all gone that route one time or another — it can be a lot of laughs, two girls and one dildo."

Nevertheless, I continued to protest our innocence, while Letitia, getting more and more drunk on gin, described in some detail how, many years before, she had been seduced by Buck Loner's wife Bobbie Dean who then, no doubt filled with remorse, got religion one day while buying Belgian endives at the Farmers Market and gave up diking on the spot to become a Jehovah's Witness. The story is not without its inspirational side.

But I am more concerned with Mary-Ann's reputation, and our relationship which means more to me than anything in this world.

I talked to Mary-Ann a few minutes ago, shortly after the dead-drunk Letitia was wheeled back to her room. Mary-Ann sounded happy. She can't wait for me to come home. I told her what the doctor told me just now: the cast comes off tomorrow and I will be able to go home by the end of the week. Unfortunately he refuses to give me a hormonal injection and my face looks a fright, with strange patches of beard. I also dread the removal of the bandage since, according to the nurse, all my lovely hair has been cut off. I hope Mary-Ann can bear the gruesome sight. I hope I can.

41

Where are my breasts? *Where are my breasts?*

42

What an extraordinary document! I have spent all morning reading this notebook and I can hardly believe that I was ever the person who wrote those demented pages. I've been debating whether or not to show them to my wife but I think, all in all, it's better to let the dead past bury its dead. As it is, neither of us ever mentions the period in which I was a woman and except for my agent, Miss Van Allen, we deliberately avoid seeing anyone who knew me in those days.

For over three years now we have been living in the San Fernando Valley on what they call a ranch but is actually just a few acres of date palms and lemon trees. The house is modern with every convenience and I have just built an outdoor barbecue pit which is much admired by the neighbors, many of whom are personalities in show business or otherwise work in some capacity or another in the Industry. Ours is a friendly community, with many fine people to share interests with.

At present I am writing a series, currently in its second year on ABC. I would of course like very much to do feature films but they are not that easy to come by. Miss Van Allen, however, keeps submitting my name so who knows when lightning will strike? Meanwhile, the series is a good credit and I make good money.

While cleaning out the attic, I came across this note-book along with all the manuscripts I wrote back in New York. Frankly I can't make head or tail of them. I certainly went through a pretentious phase! Luckily everything is now stabilized for me and I have just about the best wife and marriage I know of. Mary-Ann still sings professionally from time to time as well as appearing locally on television with her own children's program five days a week in the early A.M. She is quite a celebrity with the small fry in the Valley.

It's been a long time since I've seen Buck Loner but he's doing O.K. with the Academy, I gather, and every now and then one of the students actually gets a job in show business. So my work wasn't entirely in vain. The most famous alumnus is Ace Mann who used to be Rusty Godowsky. After mopping up in that television series, he promptly inked a multiple nonexclusive contract with Universal and is now the Number Four Box Office Star in the World, according to *Film Daily*. He is also, I'm sorry to learn, a complete homosexual, for which I feel a certain degree of responsibility and guilt. But Dr. Montag, whom I ran into last week outside Will Wright's on Santa Monica Boulevard, said he thought it was probably always in the cards for Rusty and what I did to him just brought his true nature to the surface. I hope he's right.

Dr. Montag seems happy, although he now weighs over three hundred pounds and at first I didn't recognize him, but then he didn't recognize me either. Well, none of us is getting any younger. I am now almost entirely bald, which I compensate for by wearing a rather dashing R.A.F.-style moustache. Needless to say, it is a constant sadness that Mary-Ann and I can never have children. But ever since we both became Christian Scientists we tend to believe that what happens in this life is for the best. Although I nearly lost my mind and tried to kill myself when I learned that my breasts had been removed (Dr. Mengers had been forced to take this step because my life was endangered by the silicone which, as a result of the accident, threatened to enter the bloodstream), I now realize that it was the best thing that ever happened to me if only because once Mary-Ann realized that I was really *Myron* Breckinridge, her attitude toward me changed completely. Two weeks after I left the hospital where I spent my long convalescence and rehabilitation, we were married in Vegas, and so were able at last to settle down and live a happy and a normal life, raising dogs and working for Planned Parenthood.

Incidentally, I noticed a quotation scribbled in one of the margins of the notebook. Something she (I hate to say "I"!) copied from some book about Jean-Jacques Rousseau. I don't suppose it's giving away any secrets to say that like so many would-be intellectuals back East Myra never actually read books, only books about books. Anyway the quotation still sort of appeals to me. It is about how humanity would have been a lot happier if it had kept to "the middle ground between the indolence of the primitive state and the questing activity to which we are prompted by our self-esteem." I think that is a very fine statement and one which, all in all, I'm ready to buy, since it is a proven fact that happiness, like the proverbial bluebird, is to be found in your own backyard if you just know where to look.